Loveswept® 524

Judy Gill
Golden Warrior

BANTAM BOOKS

NEW YORK · TORONTO · LONDON · SYDNEY · AUCKLAND

GOLDEN WARRIOR
A Bantam Book / February 1992

If you would be interested in receiving protective vinyl
covers for your Loveswept books, please write to this address
for information:

Loveswept
Bantam Books
P.O. Box 985
Hicksville, NY 11802

ISBN 0-553-44223-6

Published simultaneously in the United States and Canada

PRINTED IN THE UNITED STATES OF AMERICA

OPM   0 9 8 7 6 5 4 3 2 1

"You do turn me on, Sylvia," Eric said, tightening his hands on her shoulders, feeling the bones and muscles under his fingers, and the warmth and scent of her combined to threaten his sanity.

"I do?" There was a half-smile on her lips, but her eyes still held a hint of doubt. "You haven't acted, well, interested."

"I haven't? If you think that, well, then you haven't been paying attention. What did you want, for me to jump you the minute we were alone?"

She laughed, a soft, breathless sound that slid into his bloodstream and made it bubble. "Maybe not what I wanted, but it was what I . . . expected, I guess. When you didn't, I had to conclude that I'm not your type. It's okay, though. There's nothing wrong with my self-confidence. There are men whose type I am, so—"

"Sylvia." He silenced her by placing a pair of fingers across her lips. "You haven't been listening to me. There is only one thing I want more than to give you a good-night kiss," he went on, "and that is to crawl into that bed with you and give you a thousand kisses. Ever since I first saw you at the airport, I've been having fantasies about you, and me, and beds."

Her eyes were wide and searching as she stared at him. "Really?"

"Yes," he said softly, bending low over her, still holding her gaze. "Knowing all that, do you still want a good-night kiss?"

She parted her lips slightly. The tip of her tongue came out and brushed them. She took a shaky breath. Then, eyes shining with expectation and desire, she said, "Yes. . . ."

WHAT ARE *LOVESWEPT* ROMANCES?

They are stories of true romance and touching emotion. We believe those two very important ingredients are constants in our highly sensual and very believable stories in the *LOVESWEPT* line. Our goal is to give you, the reader, stories of consistently high quality that may sometimes make you laugh, sometimes make you cry, but are always fresh and creative and contain many delightful surprises within their pages.

Most romance fans read an enormous number of books. Those they truly love, they keep. Others may be traded with friends and soon forgotten. We hope that each *LOVESWEPT* romance will be a treasure—a "keeper." We will always try to publish

LOVE STORIES YOU'LL NEVER FORGET
BY AUTHORS YOU'LL ALWAYS REMEMBER

The Editors

For the Galiano Dozen
with
love and gratitude

One

For the past ten minutes the woman had captured more of Eric Lind's attention than he liked. First, her long, loose stride as she came out of the tunnel had made him look twice. Then his gaze followed her as she sought out a baggage cart and wheeled it to the carousel to load it, bending to snatch up two bags as they came around. He nodded in appreciation of the sweep of a slender thigh, the curve of her indented waist, as she waited for the third bag, which she claimed with the same brisk ease. Her hair, cut in a bell shape, hung in a sun-streaked light brown curtain past her chin, swinging out each time she bent, dipping back in toward her throat when she came erect.

Turning the cart, she came toward him, passing within a foot of where he stood while he studiously did not look at her. But a momentary whiff of her perfume trapped him into turning to watch her go—the neat, quick placement of each long, narrow foot, the swing of her legs, the subtle, sexy sway of her bottom.

With difficulty he forced his attention back to the task of searching the crowd for his friend's niece, who should have been on the same flight the woman had arrived on. Maybe she'd gone to the rest room.

The next time he saw the woman, she was standing by a row of chairs, one hand on the baggage cart, the other on her hip. Her eyes, the color of which he couldn't discern, were scanning the crowd. They lit on him, lingered, then swept on . . . and returned. This time, she met his eyes for a moment—speculatively, he thought—before looking away, and he couldn't help smiling at her. Maybe her name was April, like Rob's niece, and the sign he held kept pulling her gaze back to him. When it swept over him once more and clung for a moment, he smiled again before he could stop himself. Holy hell, this wasn't his style, coming on to a strange woman in an airport! He was here to represent Rob McGee, not emulate him. Quickly, he wrenched his gaze free, then glanced back to see her turned half away, gesturing, speaking to—possibly arguing with—someone seated out of his view on the row of chairs.

His heart went still in his chest as she fixed her gaze on his face and nodded, clearly having made up her mind about something, then marched toward him, swaying gracefully as she wove her way across the jammed concourse.

He froze where he stood. It was all right to fantasize about a woman thirty feet away. It was something else to have her approach, smiling, self-assured, looking for . . . something, because no matter what this particular woman sought, he was all too sure he'd try to find a way to provide it.

• • •

He wasn't in uniform, which was probably why April had insisted that he wasn't her uncle, in spite of the fact that he held a sign with her name on it. Sylvia's young charge hadn't seen her uncle for nearly two years, so she might not recognize him, just as the man on the far side of the concourse clearly hadn't recognized April. He'd come equipped with a sign, obviously not expecting to recognize her. Of course, there was always the possibility that Robert McGee had sent someone else, such as the man with whom he shared a house and a reputation. This man did not, in Sylvia's estimation, look the part of the quintessential roué. With his jaw carved from stone and his brows drawn together under a sweep of thick, dark hair, he did, however, look completely masculine, undoubtedly sexy, and dangerously virile.

He also, she realized when she was within a couple of feet of him, looked downright forbidding.

Sylvia lifted her chin half an inch higher and came to a halt before him. She was not in the habit of letting anybody forbid her to do anything.

With a smile, she said, "Hello, are you Major McGee?"

His eyes—mariner's eyes, she thought—were strikingly blue under those straight dark brows. He lowered the large brown hand holding the sign reading APRIL and said, "No, I'm not. I'm Eric Lind, a friend of his."

Sylvia stared at him, wondering at the depth of her disappointment. She knew now she'd been insanely hoping that he not be the housemate, one of the womanizing pair that April's grandmother held in such low esteem. And that was stupid. No matter who he was, she was here to turn April over and then leave.

As if her silence had nudged him into action, he fished his wallet out of an inside pocket in his brown leather jacket and flipped it open to show a military ID card. Heavens, but he was photogenic! Most people looked like criminals on photo IDs, but he looked like a model for a recruiting poster. "Rob asked me to meet his niece," he said, "but I was expecting someone a little younger than you."

Satisfied that he was who he said he was, she replied, "She is, I assure you. She's eight years old. I'm Sylvia Mathieson of We Deliver, Personal Courier Service." She dug in the large tapestry bag she had slung over her shoulder and came up with a card, which she handed him as she gestured to her right. "April's waiting over there."

He blinked, looked at her intently, then read aloud her company motto: "'We Deliver—Anything, Anywhere, Anytime.'" Sylvia's stomach did a back flip as amusement softened his hard mouth, crinkled the corners of his blue eyes, made them dance. "You deliver children?"

She had to laugh. He had a wonderful smile, and she decided on the spot that he looked like a man she could be friends with. Not that she'd be around long enough to strike up a friendship, but if . . . Oh, Lord, all women responded to him like this! She would not be one of a crowd!

"Not in the usual sense of the term," she said briskly. "I provide escort service for children, pets, and egg rolls, among other things."

Sylvia, Eric thought, running his thumb over the embossed letters of her name, repeating the syllables in his mind as he replayed the sound of her light laughter, struck by the very rightness of her name. A musical name to go with her musical laugh. She spoke in an intriguing voice. all husky and rough and warm. as if she'd just woken from a long and relaxing sleep. this Sylvia who had a laughing name to go with those laughing golden-brown eyes. A beautiful name to whisper in the dark and a husky voice to whisper his back to him and—

"Egg rolls?" he echoed. finally catching up with her conversational pace. and she laughed again. over her shoulder this time as she walked away. The lively brown eyes beckoned him to follow. her scent drawing him along in her wake like a *Star Trek* tractor beam.

"Well. only once." she said. "To a homesick guy on a construction crew in Tuktoyaktuk. His buddies arranged the delivery of a complete Chinese dinner for a birthday surprise. It took every microwave oven in camp to warm it up."

She stopped at a chair occupied by a small. pathetic-looking little figure with gangly arms and legs and a grubby blouse untucked from a crumpled skirt. The little girl clutched a nearly bald doll to her chest. "April. honey." Sylvia said. "this is Mr. Lind. He's your uncle's friend."

Eric stared. The child's nose was running. Her face was red. and she hiccuped as she breathed. as if she'd been crying for a long time. He hadn't been expecting someone so pathetic. or so small. not even after Sylvia Mathieson had said that April was eight years old. He'd been thinking about other things then. and had let that information slide by unremarked.

Still. seeing this very young child put a whole different light on doing a favor for a good buddy. What did he know of children? Certainly not enough to cope with a runny nose and a crying jag. "What's wrong with her?" he demanded.

"Nothing much." Sylvia said easily, sitting down on the chair next to April's and dragging the leggy little girl onto her lap, hugging her and rocking back and forth. She poked two fingers into a pocket of her oversized pink sweater and pulled out a tissue, which she held to April's nose with an admonition to blow. "She's overtired, and we had a rough flight," she went on. "She was sick a couple of times, and then she was a little upset at not finding her uncle waiting for her. When we saw you and your sign, she didn't want me to approach you, because she's been well warned about strangers. But she'll be okay now." With a neat flick of her wrist, Sylvia lobbed the tissue into a litter container six feet away, smoothed back April's hair with one long-fingered hand, making Eric's skin tingle as he watched, and asked gently, "Won't you, honey-bun?"

"I . . . want . . . my . . . grandma. I want . . . to go . . . home."

"I know you do, sweetheart, but you know Grandma's away, and in just a little while you'll be tucked into a nice warm bed and can sleep for a long time, and then you'll feel much better. Now come on and sit up. Say hello. This is Mr. Lind, and he's going to take us to Uncle Robbie."

Eric fought a dizzy sensation and sat down beside them. Us? She'd said he was going to take "us" to Uncle Robbie? Both of them? No way! It was a loud and clear gut-level protest. He wanted to grab Sylvia and run, tell her that he'd never take her anywhere near Robert McGee, that if he had his way, she wouldn't be allowed within a hundred-mile radius of the man. He'd keep her for himself, take that tall, lean body of hers into his arms, slowly undo all those little buttons and peel her out of that pink sweater, and—

April sat up and gave Eric an Inspector Clouseau impression. "Where is my Uncle Robbie? Why didn't he come like he promised?" The inspector suspected foul play. Eric was the prime candidate.

"Uh, well, he's in the hospital."

April's suspicion vanished as she nodded and came close to smiling, making herself a much more attractive child. "My Uncle Robbie's a doctor. A major. That makes him important. Are you a major too?"

Eric shook his head. "No, I'm a captain. That's not quite as important, but I drive a nicer car than he does."

April considered that and decided not to be impressed. "Uncle Robbie's going to take Cabby to the hospital and sew her up." She indicated the torn leg attachment on her singularly ugly little doll. "He said so on the phone, and we're going to Europa Park too. That's a little bit like Disneyland but not as big, but lots of fun."

"That'll be wonderful, won't it?" Sylvia patted April's thigh and spilled the child feet first off her lap as she arose. To Eric she said, "Will it take us long to get there? I'd like to hand April into her uncle's care as quickly as possible. I have a flight home to catch in a few hours."

Flight? He almost repeated the word, almost said, Don't go, but that was crazy, wasn't it? Of course she would go. She had come to deliver the child, and that done, there'd be nothing to keep her there. A woman like her would have a life, a home, probably a family, waiting for her on the other side of the world, and his fantasies were not her problem. He tried in vain to see if she wore a wedding or engagement ring.

"Excuse me?" She was speaking to him. Judging by the confused expression on her face, she'd been doing so while he wool-gathered again. Damn, what was the matter with him? By training and nature, he was used to making split-second decisions, and he'd never found himself lagging like this, dropping the conversational ball while he pondered things that had been said before, or replayed in his mind the musicality of a certain voice and dreamed of stripping a woman out of her clothes and . . .

Sylvia stared at him, seeing his eyes go vacant and dreamy again. Dammit, what was the matter with the man that he couldn't keep his mind on their mutual problem for more than two seconds? A chorus of feminine laughter drew her around. Ah! Of course. It was a tight knot of golden-blond—probably Swedish—air hostesses striding by in short skirts that had captured his lecherous attention. It was, she decided, downright insulting. If this was the way a real rake acted, the air hostesses could have him. She waved a hand in front of his glazed eyes.

"Are you with me, Mr. Lind? Did you say *in* the hospital?" she asked, her brows drawn together in concern. "Not *at* the hospital?"

Eric berated himself for his latest lapse of attention. "Sorry." He shook his head in an attempt to rattle some sense loose. "I'm afraid you heard me right. Rob was hurt yesterday, skiing in the Dolomites."

"Skiing? In the middle of June?"

"On a glacier." Eric pulled a wry face. "It was his last run, naturally, before leaving to fly home to be here in plenty of time to meet April's plane. Now he's in traction, and can't be moved for at least a week—until they make sure there's no infection. It's a compound fracture."

"The poor man," Sylvia said, frowning.

April, kneeling on a chair, tugged at Sylvia's sleeve, looking ready to cry again. "Isn't my Uncle Robbie going to come for me?"

"It seems not, sweetheart, but Mr. Lind's here."

April sat down again, her lower lip jutting. "I don't want Mr. Lind. I want my Uncle Robbie."

Eric smiled at the little girl as he crouched before her. "I know you do, April, but he's hurt his leg and can't travel right now. He called me on the phone last night and asked me to look after you. He wants you to come with me, April, and wait for him at our house." He reached out one hand to her, the other to a baggage cart near her chair. "Are these your suitcases? Shall we go now? He'll be phoning again this evening, and you can talk to him yourself then. Okay?"

"Nooo!" wailed April, flinging herself out of her chair and into Sylvia's arms again.

"Ah, sweetheart, don't cry," Sylvia crooned as she sat down with her burden, and Eric's throat tightened. There was no briskness now in the soft, husky voice; it was all warm honey and aching compassion as she cradled April, soothing her gently. Tenderly she stroked the ragged, messy hair back from the little girl's face. With one foot up on the edge of the chair opposite her, her position showed off a long, sweet curve of thigh encased in tight jeans. Eric tried not to stare, not to drool, not to want.

He paced away and left her to her task for several minutes, then spun on his heel, still hearing her soft, measured tones as she pleaded with April, explained again and again, repeating herself, clearly making no headway with the child. "Please," he said to her, leaning over to try to lift the little girl from her lap, "let me take her." His hand accidentally brushed the side of her breast, and he went rigid at the softness and warmth of her flesh, and the almost irresistible urge to touch her again.

As if she hadn't noticed, Sylvia turned half away, shielding April, looking fierce and maternal. "No," she said. "Give her a little time to get used to the idea. Don't try to push her into something she's not ready for. She's upset."

For several more minutes he sat in the chair beside them, breathing in Sylvia's scent, listening intently to her husky, raspy voice. Wild fantasies passed through his mind until he heard—with shocking clarity—that voice in the darkness next to him in bed, saying things that only a lover would say, and his body hardened accordingly. He shifted restlessly and cleared his throat, then leapt to his feet before he could disgrace himself.

"Come on now," he said brusquely. "This has gone far enough."

Gently, he undid the death-grip April had around her escort's neck, taking care not to touch Sylvia. But her smooth hair brushed his wrists, and he knew its perfume would linger on his skin for days. He lifted the resisting child and sat her upright in the chair he'd vacated, his hands on her skinny little shoulders, trying to ignore the glare Sylvia fixed on him, forcing himself to concentrate on April, on ways to reach her.

Discipline, reason—those were what he was used to dealing in, and since April hadn't responded favorably to Sylvia's attempts at cajolery, they were certainly worth a try. "Now listen, April," he said in what he knew was his best firm-but-kind tone. "You've made your point. You're not happy with the situation, and I understand that. You've had a long and difficult flight, and you miss your grandmother and feel upset that your uncle isn't here. But you're here, and I'm here, and we do have to leave this airport together. Now, we can do it agreeably, or we can do it otherwise, but we *are* going to do it. Understand?"

"Now, just a—" Sylvia began, but he raised a hand, silencing her. April stared at him as if he'd been speaking a language she didn't understand, but at least she'd stopped sniveling.

"All right," he said, standing erect. "Ready?" When she hesitated, her lower lip quivering, he said with a smile and only a hint of the impatience he was feeling, "April, believe me, you have no choice in this matter."

Dammit, neither did he. If he had his way, he'd hang around at the airport until Sylvia had to leave, maybe take her somewhere intimate for dinner, get to know her a little better, then give her his phone number so that if she were ever back this way, she could call him and . . . No! Dammit, no. He not only wouldn't do that, he couldn't do it. This was not a lady for a casual fling.

And the alternative was out of the question.

For the first time since making that decision several years before, he felt the full impact of it, felt his bachelorhood as a burden, one he wasn't sure he wanted to carry any longer. Holy hell! He had to get out of here. Now!

Drawing in a deep, steadying breath, he said, "April, you have to come with me. It's what your uncle expects of you. Now, come along. Are these your things?"

With wide, frightened eyes fixed on his face, April got to her feet, her mouth trembling, and nodded.

With a briefly triumphant look at Sylvia, Eric extended his hand toward her. "Thank you on Rob's behalf for the care and kindness you showed his niece," he said with undue formality while he struggled with the impulse to pull her hand up to his mouth and kiss her palm—for starters. He drew in a breath of her delicate scent for memory's sake and, still holding her hand, said, "Have a safe flight back." Then, in spite of all his good intentions, he heard himself ask, "I, uh, would you like some dinner before you leave?"

Sylvia was vastly tempted by those blue, blue eyes now looking deeply into hers as if he couldn't drag his gaze away. His hand was warm and calloused and large as it engulfed hers, and suddenly she knew she'd better keep this meeting as short as possible. For some reason he wasn't looking at blond stewardesses now, but at her.

Be careful what you wish for. . . .

Had she really felt piqued because he hadn't seemed to notice that she was a woman? Now that he had, she wanted to run. Eric Lind, lover-for-a-week, was not the man for her. She pulled her hand free. "No, thanks. We ate shortly before the plane landed. I think it would be better for you to get April home and settled as soon as you can."

Their gazes unlocked, and both swung down to the woebegone little girl. Eric slipped a hand around April's shoulder. "You're probably right," he said.

Lord, was she right! he thought. The sooner he

walked away from this golden-eyed woman, the better it would be for his libido. So, why wasn't he walking? Why was he gazing into those captivating eyes again, standing there like a dummy instead of walking away?

"What time does your return flight go?"

Sylvia glanced at a huge clock suspended in midair. "In about three hours."

"And when you get home? Will you be soaring off to some other foreign place?"

"I hope not," she said. "My sister's third baby is due any day now, and I'm her labor coach, so I want to be on hand." Oh, rats, why was she babbling about that? Eric Lind couldn't possibly be interested in her family's affairs. She was babbling, dammit, because she didn't want to leave, didn't want him to leave, wanted more time with him, time to get to know him, time to learn everything about him . . . *Insane!* She knew all she needed to know. The man was a rake. That diffident, half-shy charm in his eyes was surely practiced, calculated, designed to entrap women. Dammit, she would not be trapped!

Bending quickly, she brushed a kiss over April's cheek, hugged her, and said, "Bye-bye, honey-bun. It was fun traveling with you. Maybe we can do it again someday. You have a good time, now, and think of me when you're busy at Europa Park on all those neat rides."

April's breath continued to catch in her throat, but she nodded, and after a reproachful look at Sylvia, reluctantly walked away at Eric's side. Heading toward the terminal exit, she struck Sylvia as doing a wonderful "Joan of Arc on her way to the stake." Sylvia didn't know who April felt held the match, herself or Eric Lind.

A moment later she realized she was no longer watching the child but the broad back of the man in the brown leather jacket. She sighed. Lord, but he was gorgeous. The Scud Stud, plus.

She frowned, watching as April began to lag and as Eric Lind turned and spoke to her, bending low, then brushing her hair back from her face and patting her cheek gently. In a moment they walked on again, more slowly, Eric holding April's hand. Sylvia relaxed. April would be fine with him. He was a very nice man. The great lovers of the world always were.

With a sigh and a silly, futile wish that things had been different, she turned, and had nearly reached the moving ramp that would take her to the departure side of the airport when she heard a choked wail that sounded like her name. Glancing over her shoulder, she saw April pelting toward her, her face contorted. Trundling the baggage cart before him came Eric, in hot pursuit, weaving in and around passersby. Sylvia reached out an arm and captured April before she could sweep by, her hand over her mouth, eyes wild.

"I'm gonna be—"

"This way," Sylvia said quickly, rushing the child toward the door of the ladies' room. But it was much too late. Eric Lind jumped back with a muttered curse and a pained expression on his face as April cut loose, and tripped over a wheeled suitcase being towed by a portly gentleman crossing behind him, ending up flat on his back on the floor. April's baggage cart, whose handle he still held in one hand, spilled its contents onto his chest, while the child herself turned to Sylvia, accepting the handkercheif Sylvia extended with her right hand as her left hand instinctively administered a series of comforting pats.

"Are you all right?" Sylvia stared at the recumbent man, saw him struggle with anger, resentment, and other emotions, then saw amusement conquer all as he laughed and waved away the assistance offered by the man whose suitcase had tripped him. Shoving April's luggage off him, he regained his feet with lithe grace.

"I'm sorry, Sylvia. I'm sorry," April said, her head hanging as she shivered with reaction. "I tried not to get sick, but I felt really bad in my tummy, and when I told Mr. Lind, he said I'd be fine if I just breathed in through my nose and out through my mouth, nice and steady, and kept on walking."

"It works for me when I feel airsick," Eric explained, haphazardly replacing the suitcases in the cart.

Sylvia stared at him, incredulous. "You're in the air force, for heaven's sake! You can't get airsick."

"Unless I'm at the controls, I do. You think putting on a uniform is some kind of magic cure?"

"You think breathing through your mouth is?"

"As I said, it works for me." Then, with a half-shrug and another charmingly self-conscious grin, he added, "Most of the time."

"It didn't work for me." April sniffled, impervious to his charm. From the shelter of Sylvia's encircling arm, she looked miserably at Eric's splattered shoes. "Please don't be mad at me, Mr. Lind. I didn't do it on purpose."

"Honey, I'm not mad at you."

"You cussed," she said.

He looked apologetic. "I know, and I'm sorry about that. I was . . . startled. I know you couldn't help it. I would have preferred you to run to a rest room rather than to Sylvia, but . . . any port in a storm, I guess."

Yup. He looked into Sylvia's calm, light brown eyes, and he knew that if he were caught in a storm, he might seek a port like her. As if sensing the direction his thoughts were taking, she looked down quickly, and he was surprised to see a gentle flush rise up on her cheeks. Now what, he wondered, brought that on? Surely the woman couldn't really read minds.

Sylvia's breath caught in response to something in Eric Lind's gaze. Honestly, there had to be something wrong with her head, the way she responded so swiftly to a man like him. Grinding her teeth, she cursed the vivid imagination that wanted her to believe he had never looked at another woman in exactly the same way he was looking at her. She was crazy!

"Of course you couldn't help it," she said to the child, giving her a quick hug before propelling her toward the rest room. "Be right back," she said to Eric, and over her shoulder saw him digging in his pocket for a tip to give the cleaner who had appeared as if by magic. Good, she thought. Serves him right for rushing April out before she was ready to go.

She sighed as she tidied the little girl. She had to be fair and admit that what had happened was as much her fault as it was Eric Lind's. She'd known April was too upset to make the transition easily. She should have accepted the man's offer of dinner to give April more time to get to know him, but she'd wanted to flee as fast as possible, before she went into any more tailspins looking into Eric Lind's incredible eyes.

Why does he have to be so damned nice? she

wondered. Why is the man so totally attractive when it's all sham? No, that wasn't fair either. His charm was genuine, his attractiveness real, and if he chose to spread it around the world, offering it to all comers, it didn't mean the charm was less real—only that it was less . . . valuable.

Her main concern was April McGee, not herself and her own suddenly jagged and confused feelings about Eric Lind, so there was no need for her to run away in a panic just because she was attracted to him. All she needed to do was remember that he wore his winning ways as he did his uniform—as a way of life—and that both of those factors put him off limits to her.

She'd signed a contract with April's grandmother to turn the child over to a loving uncle, and if she turned her over to someone else, especially when the child didn't want to go, she'd be in dereliction of duty.

With her decision made, she marched April out of the ladies' room, but at the sight of Eric Lind's carved-in-stone chin, and her foolish response to what his blue eyes did to her insides, she nearly changed her mind again. She concentrated on April's small, trusting hand gripping hers tightly and tilted her head up high to meet his gaze. He was tall, but so was she, and with the heels of her shoes affording her an extra few inches, their eyes were almost on a level. So, she noted, were their mouths, but squelched the thought even as it formed.

She might find that hard-looking, chiseled male mouth fascinating, she might wonder what it would feel like on hers, but she would never know, so it was better not to let herself get caught up in any erotic daydreaming. Instead, she had to focus on the matter at hand, and battle it out with him if need be.

"I'm going with you," she said without preamble, and watched him take a quick step back, paling as if she'd jammed rigid fingers into his solar plexus.

Two

"What?" Eric's voice was strained, hoarse, horrified, Sylvia thought. Clearly, he saw her only as a complication, excess baggage he didn't want on hand. Of course. A visiting child might put a minor cramp in his style. A visiting child with an adult female companion could make managing his kind of love life extremely awkward.

That, though, was not her problem. She repeated her words. "I'm going with you and April."

April's face glowed as she tugged on Sylvia's hand, looking up at her. "You are? To Uncle Robbie's house? Honest?"

"You betcha," Sylvia said with conviction. She hadn't had any vacation yet this year, and Janine could easily take over for a week or so. "I know when I'm needed and where I'm needed, and I'm not going to leave you until you're completely comfortable about your situation or your uncle gets home, whichever comes first."

"Yaaay!" April's shriek of joy nearly deafened her, but Sylvia didn't care; it was worth it to see the little girl return to her smiling, enthusiastic self.

"But . . . I can't—You can't—" Eric began, then broke off, caught up in the web of her spell as she smiled at him, kindly, so very kindly, and with complete understanding. Oh, Lord, what did she understand? How could she understand any of this when he didn't? Had he somehow given away his massive confusion about her?

"I can't, in all conscience, leave a scared and lonely child in the hands of a man she doesn't know, and doesn't want to accompany," she said.

Eric felt sweat break out on his upper lip, along his spine. She meant it. He looked into those golden-brown eyes of hers and knew she meant every word of it. The world shifted under his feet. He didn't know if this was a dream come true, or a nightmare about to begin. For the sake of his own sanity, he'd envisioned this woman on a west-bound plane, diminishing as she was whisked away, fading from his memory, her musical laughter a dwindling echo, but if she stayed, if he got to know her . . . Oh, Lord! Help! From the moment he'd seen her, he'd had a sick, sinking sensation that this was the one woman in the world who might be able to weaken all his strong convictions about what was right and what was wrong and what, even, was possible. . . .

He shook his head as he stared at her. "What . . . what about your flight?"

She shrugged. "What about it? There'll be other flights."

"Your sister," he said, wildly casting about for ways to change her mind because he knew very well that if she stayed, it wouldn't be in some cold, impersonal hotel. "Her baby. You wanted to be there."

He saw her hesitate, saw a cloud cross her face

momentarily. Then she wiped it away with a bright smile. "As I said, it's her third, and our other sister will probably take over. Besides, Jasmine has a husband—it's not as if she'll be alone. Not the way April will be if I abandon her."

A faint sheen of perspiration was filming his forehead. She couldn't mean what she was saying, couldn't intend to come and stay in his house, sleep under his roof, take off all her clothes and . . .

Clothes! "You don't have any baggage," he observed.

Again, she shrugged. She patted her tapestry bag. "I have a change of underwear and a toothbrush. I never travel without them, and I believe there are a couple of stores in Germany? Would it be too much trouble for you to search out one of them and turn me loose for twenty minutes? I could shop here, of course," she went on, gesturing toward a display window where a lot of fancy lingerie hung wispily on angular mannequins. "But I prefer not to pay airport prices unless I have to."

"I . . . uh . . ." Eric stepped back another pace from her. Twenty minutes? He forced himself to focus on that rather than think about her in one of those wispy negligees. Or out of it. "What woman can shop for clothes in twenty minutes?"

"I tend to make up my mind in a hurry," she said dryly.

That was one thing they had in common, then, considering the way his mind had made itself up about her—or at least the way his body had. He swallowed hard and said hoarsely, "You can do this? Just up and decide to stay in a foreign country?"

"Sure. No visa required here," she said, her golden gaze wide and candid on his, her face bracketed by two paler streaks of hair that fell from where her double cowlicks pushed it up and back from her brow.

"I don't mean that. I meant your business." He frowned. Her card had listed her as not only the owner but also the managing director of We Deliver. "Don't you have commitments?"

What he really wanted to know was did she have a man who'd come flying over here to see what was going on if she didn't go back on that return flight of hers and who'd take Eric apart when he found Sylvia living in *his* house, sleeping in *his* bed and . . . Holy hell, why couldn't he get a handle on this thing? This woman was not going to "live" in his house, not in that sense, and certainly was not going to sleep in his bed! Like every other woman that came through the front door of his house, she'd be sleeping in Rob's bed, and unlike the others, she'd be doing it alone—at least until Rob got back. Then, the situation would be up for grabs.

"Nothing that can't be shunted onto my best assistant," she said, and he had to think hard for a minute to remember where the conversation had been when he'd left it for his little flight of fancy.

Eric stood irresolute for several more seconds. What could he do? Clearly, with the matter taken out of his hands like this by an impetuous woman, there wasn't a hell of a lot of room for him to maneuver, was there? Briefly, he recognized that it wasn't in his nature simply to let things happen to him. He not only liked to be in charge but needed to be; yet since he'd seen a golden-eyed woman come striding toward him across an airport concourse, a lot of things had changed, and while he might be a captain in the air force, a man accustomed to being in command, he was no longer captain of his own fate. Hell, he wasn't even captain of his own damned canoe!

"Then . . . then I guess there's nothing more to say," he said helplessly, and shrugged.

That shrug, and his cool, aloof, uncaring expression told Sylvia that he'd decided to make the best of a bad situation. It rankled. She was not accustomed to being considered a "bad situation." She had to let him know that she wasn't here for a good time, that she wouldn't expect anything of him simply because he had a reputation as a stud.

She could carry it off. Cool, friendly, and confident. That was the way to go—simply act natural, be herself. After all, since it was clear that she didn't do anything for him, why should he be allowed to guess that he could turn her inside out with nothing more than a smile? There were plenty of men who thought she was more than just okay; she didn't need to feel bad or inadequate because this one, who was undoubtedly accustomed to what Mrs. Anderson had called "loose European women" fawning over him, hadn't tried to put the make on her.

"Thank you," she said, her smile widening, her teeth, white and even, flashing.

Eric wanted to kiss her so badly, he thought he might explode with the feeling. Oh, Lord, this was getting worse, not better.

"Since I'm staying," she went on airily, "I'll need to make a phone call. And could you provide a number where I can be reached? I'll keep the call short, because April is about to fall asleep leaning on my hip."

• • • •

"Umm," Sylvia said fifteen minutes later after having spoken to her mother, who would pass a message on to her office, "I love Alfa Romeos." This was a large one, she noticed, not a sports job but a four-door sedan, and was very, very opulent. After making sure April was secure in the back, she got in and ran a hand over the edge of the seat, smiling at Eric as he prepared to shut her door. "And the scent of leather." The June sun had shone on the leather, warming it, and she settled herself in, clicked her seat belt, and leaned back, smiling out over the long maroon hood of the car as Eric drove the sedan out of the airport area and then shot forward into the breathtakingly fast traffic of the Autobahn.

They were quiet for some minutes, both lost in private thoughts, but Eric feared *his* thoughts would become less than private if he couldn't curb his imagination. Lord, when she'd stroked the leather of the seat, it was as if she'd stroked him and his body had responded exactly as nature had planned. When she stretched, getting comfortable, her firmly sculpted breasts thrust forward, straining the buttons of her sweater . . . to say nothing of the zipper in his pants. He swallowed, trying not to look at her even for an instant, but he didn't have to look to be totally aware of her. Her scent hovered around him, and somehow her warmth reached over to where he sat behind the wheel and brought sweat to his upper lip again. He'd have taken off his jacket, but it covered him, keeping him moderately decent.

She glanced over her shoulder and said, "Would you look at that? April's out cold already. It was thoughtful of you to bring a blanket and pillow for her. I was hoping she'd sleep as soon as she relaxed, which she didn't do on the plane."

Eric risked a glance at Sylvia. "You seem very relaxed too. A lot of . . . people . . . are nervous traveling at this speed."

She laughed. "Now, why do I get the impression you were about to say 'women' instead of 'people,' but very tactfully changed it?"

He had to laugh with her. It was nice, hearing the two sounds blend, he thought. "Probably because that is what I almost said, but I'm told by the experts—Rob McGee, primarily—that women hate to hear generalizations like that about themselves."

"As a generalization, it may be true," she said, "but personally, I love speed. I find it exciting."

"Exciting, hmm?" he asked, and when she nodded, egging him on, he passed a Mercedes and a BMW as if they were standing still. "Then let's go," he said. "There's no speed limit here." He felt a huge smile split his face as he glanced at her and saw that she was truly enjoying the thrill of the speed. He himself enjoyed her response to it, the way her white teeth bit into her bottom lip, the way she gripped the sides of the seat as he let the car leap ahead on a long, straight, open stretch of road. Her eyes danced, shining brightly, her cheeks flushed, and she threw her head back as if the car were open and she could feel the wind rush in her hair. Oh, Lord, but he wished the Alfa were a convertible, he wished they were alone, he wished he could excite her in a hundred other ways!

Sylvia laughed in delight as the needle swept up the speedometer's face, and when he slowed to a more sedate speed she said wistfully, "I don't suppose you'd let me drive your car, would you? I have an international license."

Eric laughed again and switched back to the right-hand lane in response to a set of flashing headlights coming up rapidly behind him. "I don't suppose I would either. I don't even let Rob drive my Alfa."

Sylvia nodded, feeling her crazy excitement drop with the speed as she suppressed a sigh. Rob. The other half of the Dreadful Duo, the Predatory Pair, the Reckless Rakes. Right. She should thank him for the reminder. As charming as this man was, as much as a moment of warm, shared laughter and a burst of speed from a powerful car under his superb control could thrill her, he was not for her. He might pretend that Rob McGee was the expert on women and himself out of Rob's league, but she mustn't be taken in by his disingenuous remarks.

"How did you end up escorting April?" Eric asked, wanting her to speak again so that maybe he could analyze her voice and discover what, exactly, it displayed that appealed so strongly to him. "I mean, I understood that her grandmother was to come with her."

"That's right. She and her new husband planned a honeymoon trip through the Alps before taking a Mediterranean cruise. But April's new step-grandpa, Mr. Anderson, developed an ear infection a couple of days before the wedding, and his doctor said it would be too painful for him to fly. Luckily, their cruise doesn't start for another week and a half, but instead of waiting for his ear to clear up, they managed to book passage on a freighter headed this way. April and her uncle haven't seen each other in a couple of years, and Mrs. Anderson knew he'd taken leave just for this occasion, so it was imperative to get her here, and that's where I came in."

"I see. Rob didn't tell me any of this. He simply mentioned a couple of weeks ago that his niece would be coming to stay." Actually, Rob seldom spoke of his family, and Eric, for his part, wouldn't have been greatly interested if he'd offered more information.

"Have you and Major McGee known each other a long time?"

"About ten years," he said. "We went through officer training together, and have ended up on the same base quite a number of times."

"Are you a doctor too?"

"Not a chance!"

"You sound horrified at the thought."

He smiled. "It takes a special sort of person to be a doctor." Sylvia heard a hint of regret. "Rob's that type, and I'm the opposite."

"What kind of man is the opposite of the kind it takes to be a doctor?"

"A doctor heals," he said on a slightly bitter note, an oblique answer if she'd ever heard one. She didn't know why, since they were barely acquainted, but she wanted honesty from this man, not equivocations. Fool that she was, she wanted, she thought, for him to treat her differently than he did all the other women in his life. All women wanted that from all men, and seldom got it.

"I know that," she said. "But what do you consider to be the opposite of a healer?"

"A killer?" He only seemed to be asking. In spite of the intonation, Sylvia thought he was making a deliberately provocative statement.

She gazed at his set profile until he took his eyes

off the road long enough to meet her assessing stare. "I don't think you're that," she said.

He shrugged, turning his attention back to traffic. "Why not? It's my job, what I'm trained to do. I'm a pilot."

"I'm guessing you don't fly transport," she said quietly. And guessing a whole lot more, besides. He was hurting. Something preyed on his mind.

He shrugged again and was quiet for several moments, then said, "I was in the Persian Gulf." He didn't add *during the war*, but he didn't have to.

"I'm sorry," Sylvia said. "I don't suppose it was pleasant."

He frowned. "It wasn't all bad. Most of what I did was fly escort for U.S. bombers and dodge stuff coming up at us from the ground, since there was little, if any, enemy interference from the air. We also provided air cover over the Allied fleet at sea in the Gulf. Toward the end, though," he added, almost defiantly, she thought, "we flew some air-to-ground sorties. So yes, though I didn't see the results personally, I suppose that makes me a killer."

"That's what happens in a war."

He flicked another look over her, his eyes registering surprise. "You don't sound particularly disgusted. Or impressed."

She shook her head. "I'm neither." That wasn't entirely true. She *was* impressed with this man, for a lot of reasons, none of which she should be dwelling on unless she could content herself with a purely platonic relationship. Anything more would simply be too dangerous. She'd only just begun to realize she was fully healed from a disastrous relationship with a man who'd turned out to be a charming womanizer. She didn't need another Don Juan in her life.

"Most women are one or the other, if you'll forgive another generalization," he said. "I seem to make a habit of them, but in a way, so do a lot of women when it comes to jet jocks. They see fighter pilots as either heroes or monsters, nothing in between."

Curious, she asked, "Do you really care what women think?" Experience had taught her that professional Lotharios seldom did.

He quirked a half-smile in her direction. "Now that you mention it, I guess maybe I do. I care what people think. People I might like to have as . . . friends."

Dammit. Until now, he hadn't really cared what anybody thought, male or female, but it was important that Sylvia Mathieson not think him a monster. On reflection, he decided he wasn't even certain he wanted her to see him as a hero. It would, he thought, be preferable for her to think of him simply as a man. A man she might be interested in—for more than friendship.

But no. She'd be in his life a few days only, and that was best. Best, hell! It was the only way possible for him. He would not drag a woman into the kind of life he'd chosen for himself, the way his father had done with his mother—ultimately destroying her, along with his offspring's childhood. It wouldn't be fair.

He wished he could be like Rob, and fall in and out of love every month or two, never take anything or anyone very seriously. Rob didn't think about life, maybe because he saw death so often in his profession, and the women in his orbit were of the same nature: freewheeling, happy-go-lucky, living for the day—and the night—ahead, with little thought for any kind of future.

What kind of woman, he wondered, stealing a glance at Sylvia's face, was she? Did she dream of the future, and if so, what did those dreams entail? Certainly not a man who might not even have a future to share with her.

"Tell me about yourself."

They spoke the words together, and then laughed, again together. Reaching across the seat with his free hand, Eric covered hers as it lay relaxed beside her.

He had nice hands, hard, not soft. She disliked being touched by a man with soft hands as much as she disliked being kissed by a man with limp lips. Dammit, there she went again, thinking about kissing him!

"Ladies first," he said.

She gently disengaged her hand from his clasp. "Okay," she said. "Where do you want me to begin?"

"As far back as you can remember."

"Ah," she said. "Well, you asked for it." She paused dramatically, then began in a sepulchral voice. "It was dark in there, and wet, and there was tremendous pressure, forcing me down a long, tight tunnel. . . ."

Eric's shout of laughter cut into her story before he remembered that April was sleeping in the backseat. More softly, but still chuckling, he said, "You don't remember back that far!"

"No? How can you be sure? What's your first memory?"

Without hesitation, he said, "Of my mother, screaming."

"Why was she screaming?"

"I don't think I knew at the time, but my sister, who's ten years older, told me later that was the day the news came that our father had bought it somewhere over Cold Lake, Alberta, on a training flight."

This time, it was she who reached out and took his hand. "I'm sorry," she said. "How old were you?"

"Three, nearly four, I think."

"How sad for her. For all of you. Is it difficult for her, knowing you're flying?"

He smiled, a bitter twisting of his lips as he slid his hand out from under hers on the gearshift lever and clamped it hard around the steering wheel. "She doesn't know."

"I'm sorry. When did you lose her?"

"When? That day, I suppose. As I said, she screamed, and she didn't stop screaming until they gave her a shot. Every time the sedation wore off, she screamed again. Finally, she did stop, but by then she'd stopped talking, too, stopped functioning—stopped living, I guess. My sister, Olivia, and I were raised by an aunt and uncle."

A certain heaviness belied the matter-of-fact tone in which he related the way he was raised, and why. Such loss at an early age couldn't be easy to overcome. Her heart ached for any child who grew up with a single parent, but to think of one losing both was almost more than she could bear.

"Didn't your mother ever get well?" she asked.

He shook his head and signaled a lane change, moving out to pass a stream of traffic.

"Not really," he said, when he'd guided the car back to the right. "She did come out of the hospital for a number of years, and lived with us in her sister's home, but she was never our mother again, not in any meaningful way. She's in a nursing home now, in the countryside near Kingston, Ontario, where she's happy, in a vague sort of way. She knits a lot, and crochets, and does some very delicate little watercolors of pretty ponds with pink flowering trees and weeping willows and swans; gentle, safe places. I think that's the world she prefers to live in. When she sees me, though, she cries and calls me Charlie, my dad's name. I don't see her very often."

After a time, Sylvia said, "It must be terribly hard."

"I don't think so, and I'm grateful for that. My aunt and uncle and sister all live close to her. Livvy's married and has two daughters and a son, all teenagers. They spend a lot of time with Mother—she goes to their house for dinner every Sunday and on holidays. She's not lonely."

"I didn't mean hard for her. I meant for you."

"No."

He denied it with a thrust of his chin that left Sylvia feeling shut out, as if she'd probed too deeply.

Chastened, Sylvia watched the scenery flash by, blinking in surprise when she saw, on a distant hilltop, a castle. "Look!" she said. "An honest-to-goodness castle. Oh, it has turrets and a flag flying. Does that mean the king or the baron or whatever is in residence?"

"No. It means it's open to rake in the tourist shekels," he said with a grin. "We could take a drive in a day or two, and you could have a closer look at some of the castles in the neighborhood," he offered.

"Thank you. I'd like that. But don't you have to work?"

He shook his head. "I'm due some leave, so I can probably arrange a few free days now. Rob made plans for some tours and activities for his niece—I'll carry them out instead."

She settled back in her seat and watched the land slip by, fascinated by everything she saw; it all had a different flavor and texture about it, a delicious foreignness, which wasn't surprising, of course.

Then, as if thinking aloud, remembering, Eric broke the silence again.

"The first time my mother saw me in uniform—the only time—she screamed again, like she did the day Dad went west. And every time I see her, I sort of hold my breath, afraid it'll happen again, though I've never worn my uniform to the home since that day. I'm a coward, I guess—to the point that for a long time I had to force myself to go visit her."

"Yes." His eyes flicked sideways, startled—and, she thought, hurt. She said, "Not 'Yes, I think you're a coward,' but 'Yes, I think I'd avoid that kind of pain too.'"

After a moment, he said, "Want to hear something really lousy about me?"

"If you want to tell me."

He sighed. "This four-year posting out of the country gave me a feeling of freedom I hadn't enjoyed in a long time. I go back once or twice a year, and it's a relief to see her so seldom."

"Yes," she said again.

"Is that all you have to say?" he asked aggressively. "Don't you want to tell me I'm a washout as a son?"

She shook her head. "No."

"Well, I am. As a nephew too." He sat deep in

thought for a time, then went on, speaking into the silence, not looking at Sylvia. "None of them wanted me to follow in my father's footsteps, but from the time I could walk, I think I wanted to fly."

He smiled then and met her gaze for a split second, and her heart tumbled over. "You know, I do have another memory at that, an earlier one, and a happier one. A man, probably my father, tossing me high in the air, telling me I was flying. I got so excited, I nearly wet myself. I remember my mother laughing and scolding him and rushing me off to the bathroom. Yet even after I learned better bladder control, that wild, excited sensation came back if I so much as thought about soaring high above the world."

"Maybe something like that can be in a person's blood, inherited like blue eyes or brown hair."

"Maybe." He ran a hand over his thick, dark hair. "For sure environment didn't play a big part in my final choice, though I tried to be a good nephew to my uncle, to the extent of saying—and believing for a long time—that I wanted to be a dentist just like him."

Sylvia smiled. She simply couldn't see Eric Lind peering into people's mouths, talking about gum disease and urging the use of dental floss. What good would farseeing mariner's eyes—airman's eyes, Sylvia corrected herself—be in such close quarters? "What changed your mind?"

"When I was fourteen, an air force officer came to my school on Careers Day. Maybe it was the uniform, and a long-forgotten memory of my father, but to me, that man looked like a god, and from that moment on, I wanted to be like him." His bluer-than-blue eyes gazed out over the stream of traffic weaving in and out as it climbed a long hill up ahead as if he yearned to break loose of the earth and its overcrowded roads, to sweep away to freedom.

"So you joined the air force. Right out of high school?"

He shook his head swiftly. "Lord, no. The minute I mentioned it, my family went berserk. I compromised on private flying lessons paid for with money I earned summers driving farm machinery, and I even hid those lessons from my aunt and uncle, though Olivia knew, and sweated it out every time she knew I was flying. Finally, I quit telling her when I was going up. By the time I got out of college—with a degree in computer science, not dentistry—I'd learned I couldn't spend the rest of my life sitting at a keyboard, staring at a monitor."

He grinned, stretched, and flexed his hands, which had been gripping the wheel too tightly. "So now I spend my life sitting in a cockpit staring at a heads-up display, but at least I love it."

"And that's what counts, isn't it?" Sylvia asked.

"Yes," he said. "It counts for a great deal. I—" He broke off, frowning, then gave her an inquiring glance. "How the hell did you manage that? I must have used the word 'I' about a hundred times in the past half hour, and you were supposed to go first."

Sylvia laughed. "I did, remember?"

"But I still don't know anything about you, and I bored you with my life's history. Why didn't you stop me?" He sounded angry and appalled.

"Because I wasn't bored." She hadn't been, had found his story, his attitudes, his opinions, vastly interesting, and she liked the sound of his voice, too, melting over her like warm molasses, thick and rich and dark brown. This was crazy. She was taking far too great a personal interest in the man, and it had to stop. "I wasn't bored in the least."

"Thank you for that," he said with a reluctant chuckle. "Now, after your horrendous trip through the birth canal, what happened?"

"Do you know," she said with a great show of indignation, "that our society expects every tiny infant born to know automatically how to breathe, without so much as one free, introductory lesson? And if they don't figure it out immediately, they get whacked! I tell you, it's a national crime, and it should be brought to the attention of the authorities. Maybe Amnesty International could look into it. Or UNICEF. What do you think?"

Three

Eric felt young and lighthearted as he laughed again. "I think you're evading telling me about yourself." He felt rather abashed at how much *he* had confided in *her*, though at the time it had been a sweet relief to unburden himself to her sympathetic attentiveness.

She heaved a dramatic sigh, and he gulped as he wrenched his eyes from the rising and falling of her breasts. "You're on to me."

The phrase was ill-advised. What he wanted to do was come on to her hard and fast and strong, overwhelm her before she could raise any kind of defense. He was within sixty seconds of pulling his car down an off-ramp and seeking out a quiet little pension somewhere and calling it a day. Rob would have done it without hesitation and gotten away with it. But he wasn't Rob.

He swallowed hard and forced himself back into the conversation. "Did you have such a terrible childhood, Sylvia?" And if she had, would she want to talk about it with a stranger? The fact that *he* didn't feel she was a stranger didn't mean she felt the same way about him. Damn, but he was an insensitive jerk! "I'm sorry," he said. "I shouldn't have asked you that. Ignore me. I'm being a boor. You don't have to tell me anything if it's too painful."

Sylvia laughed softly and patted his hand. "You really are a sweet man," she said, and then wished she could recall the words, because he blushed and looked distinctly uncomfortable. What was wrong with her? He probably thought "sweet man" was an insult, a slur on his sexual prowess! It was enough that he felt she'd tricked him into talking about his past. That was likely something he hid from potential conquests because it showed him as much too human, not the superhero jet jock he probably portrayed himself to be. But then, his telling her about it simply proved that he did not see her as a potential conquest, pointed up the fact that she simply wasn't his type.

Unaccountably, a long, heartfelt sigh escaped her.

"My childhood wasn't painful in any way," she said, suddenly becoming aware that he was waiting for her to speak, "and if I'm avoiding talking about it, it's because I don't want to bore you to death."

Bore him? When she spoke in that intriguing voice that soaked into his bones and vibrated in all sorts of interesting places? "You won't bore me."

"Okay, then, if you're sure . . ." She paused long enough for him to tell her to forget it, and when he didn't, went on.

"I have two parents, two sisters, a"—she broke off, coughed into her cupped hands, then continued—"a . . . full complement of grandparents, all still living, various aunts and uncles and cousins, and I suffered no terrible childhood traumas, not even any really bad moments, growing up. Unless you count losing Googly on a bus."

Childhood, she told herself. *We're talking about childhood here.*

"Googly?"

"My teddy bear. Named so for his one eye, a huge button my Grandma Severn sewed on after the dog chewed him up. Mom threw him in the garbage and promised me a new one, but Grandma, who was visiting us at the time, rescued him because she couldn't stand the fuss." She remembered that fuss, in stereo. What hurt her hurt Shane, and vice versa. Three years, and she still couldn't bear to so much as mention his name.

"There wasn't enough left of the right side of his head for a button," she went on quickly, speaking over the tautness in her throat, hoping it would go away if she just kept talking, "so she patched him up as best she could and gave him one big, googly left eye. Grandma Severn's a better gardener than she is a seamstress, but she meant well and she knew how important that bear was to me." *To both of us. Oh, heaven help me, I'm going to cry!*

Eric smiled, envisioning a one-eyed, half-headed bear, inexpertly mended, and Sylvia loving it anyway. Giving her a quick look, he was amazed to see tears standing out in her eyes. "Tears over a teddy bear?" he asked, just managing to restrain himself, wanting to catch one of those tears on his fingertip and touch his tongue to it, taste her for the first time.

She sniffed, giggled, and dashed her tears away. The sound of her giggle, light and girlish and clear, delighted him as much as her husky, musical laugh and her unique, kitten-tongue voice.

"Silly, isn't it?" Sylvia asked. "I often grow what my mother likes to call 'lachrymose' when I'm overtired. My mom likes words." *Why aren't you telling him?* she asked herself. *Why are you doing this? Why pretend?* And the answer came swiftly: *Because I'm so ashamed, and I never want him to know.*

Eric knew he should tell her to curl up and go to sleep, but he wanted to keep her talking, keep her smiling, keep her laughing, purely for his own pleasure. "What was he called before he got the googly eye?" he asked.

"Teddy," she said, her tone suggesting his imagination needed work.

He groaned. "Teddy. Right."

"See, I told you," she said. "Boringly normal." One slim shoulder lifted, and as it dropped, the sleeve of her pink sweater fell loosely over her hand. She pushed the sleeve up to her elbow, baring a slender forearm with a big, daisy-faced plastic watch with a bright yellow strap around her wrist. The whimsical accessory made him want to laugh again. It made him want to hug her tightly, too, and kiss her until he turned blue. He'd never known a woman who wore a daisy for a watch. He'd never known a woman who could get teary-eyed over a teddy bear. He'd never known a woman who made him feel like this, light-headed and lighthearted and scared to death but loving it. He was beginning to suspect that he'd never known a woman, period, and was insanely, inordinately glad. He had spent his entire thirty-five years waiting for Sylvia Mathieson.

"What are you, the oldest, youngest, middle?" he

asked, wanting to know every little thing about her. Did she like peanut butter, what size were her feet, had she had her appendix out, and how did she feel about Willie Nelson and Beethoven?

"Middle. Jasmine's a year older, Sidney a year younger. We loved each other as children, fought like Kilkenny cats, as Grandpa Mathieson put it—and would have killed to protect each other. And nothing's changed. Dad was in the army until I was fifteen, when he got out and joined the Royal Canadian Mounted Police. He retired a few months ago because they wanted to ship him off to Regina and the Academy to train recruits. He and Mom didn't want to leave the Vancouver area after staying there for eight years. They live on the North Shore with a fantastic view of the harbor, the inlet, and the city."

He didn't want to know about her parents and their view. He wanted to know about her. "Did you move a lot when you were a child? That can't have been boring."

"It wasn't, and we did live in lots of places, but we always took our things with us, so Mom made each home look pretty much like the last one. She was a real milk-and-cookies mom," she said with a fond smile. "And still is. Always there for us. She's great, my mom. Writes bad poetry that I love to read because it rhymes and has a definite rhythm and tells a real story, like an old song."

Eric wanted to hear her musical voice go on and on; to him, it sounded as good as old-fashioned poetry. When she didn't continue, he said, "You call that bad poetry? It's the kind I like too."

"*I* don't call it bad, but other poets do, and publishers. You know, the deadly serious literary types? The ones who make the rules. They want obscure stuff with meaning so deeply layered in symbolism you have to dig it out with a rock pick, and even then you might be wrong, but nobody can tell you because the poet himself probably doesn't know."

She sounded so aggrieved he had to ask, "Do you write poetry too? The kind that rhymes?"

She laughed. "Not me. I barely scraped through any English course I ever took. My favorite class was phys ed, though I love to read for entertainment. But Jasmine . . . well, she's fantastically talented that way."

She turned her glowing, golden-brown eyes on him, melting his insides as she smiled with such love for her sister that he felt momentarily jealous. "She says if she ever stops reproducing long enough, she might settle down and do some serious writing, but for now, she keeps her hand in by writing letters to the editors of papers all over the country, and gets them published every time. She's a real political activist."

"She's the one who's having the baby?"

"That's right. And she'll probably be writing a letter in the delivery room, commenting on the disgraceful state of the medical system.

"Jazz has Mom's talent for words, but Sidney inherited her personality. She's Mom all over again; got married first, though she's the youngest. She was only twenty, but very much in love, and marriage to Randy was all she'd wanted since she was seventeen. They have four little girls—two sets of twins. The older pair are five and a half, the younger pair are three. Jasmine is having her third, as I said, any day now. Her little girls are four and nearly three."

"All girls?"

"All girls."

He thought of all those little replicas of Sylvia and was charmed. "And you all live close to one another?"

"Jazz and Donald bought a house only three blocks from Mom and Dad, Sidney and Randy live a ten-minute drive away."

"And you? You live with your parents?"

"No." She yawned again and stretched, then curled on the seat within the confines of her safety belt, facing him. "But I go home when I'm hungry for something special, and not always food. Sometimes, simply a hug will do, and I spend a lot of time with my nieces, who are wonderful children. I love kids, don't you?"

It must have been a rhetorical question, because she rushed on, "They're so open and honest about everything, especially before they start school. I've often thought that if I ever have children, I'll try to educate them myself so they won't have to go to school and learn to lie."

"Where do you live?"

"In a tiny downtown apartment that's as expensive as sin, but I like to be where the action is."

"What kind of action?"

"You know: close to theaters, museums, nightclubs, the beaches, Stanley Park, my office . . . whatever. I run for a few miles every morning along the seawall in the park."

He didn't want to think of her and all that "action." Nightclubs? Theaters? Whom did she go with—someone special, or whoever happened along? He didn't know which idea he disliked most.

"Do you get escort jobs like this very often?"

"They make up the bulk of my business. With so

many marriages breaking up and parents living thousands of miles apart from their children, there's a real need for this kind of personal service. Airlines are very good about looking after kids traveling alone, but they won't take them under a certain age, and even when the kids are older, a lot of parents can't stand the agony of worry such travel entails. So, if the mom, say, can't leave her job to take Jill or Johnny to Daddy's house, they hire me to make the flight with the child, and often I go and bring the same child home again."

And probably have dinner with the grateful daddy, he thought, clenching his teeth. Knock it off, Lind, he told himself briskly, then nearly groaned as he heard the words "And then there's the egg-roll crowd" pop out of his mouth.

"That was a lot of fun," Sylvia said with a chuckle. "They even invited me to share their dinner and the birthday party, since I couldn't get a flight out until the next day."

"I'm sure they did," he muttered, speaking just under the sound of Sylvia's next yawn. She patted her mouth with the back of her hand.

"Sorry, I didn't get that."

"It wasn't important." His voice was hoarse. What else had they invited her to share, those lonely men living and working at the top of the world with nothing but ice and snow and walruses for company? Oh, hell, it was none of his business!

She uncurled her legs and stuck them out in front of her, her ankles crossed, her thighs close together, smooth and long and tapering.

"You're beginning to wilt, aren't you?" he asked contritely when she stretched again, exposing a long length of creamy, vulnerable throat.

"No, no. I'm fine," she said. "But I'd give my back teeth for a three-mile jog."

No, he thought. Sleep was what she needed. What kind of man was he, keeping her awake when she needed sleep. He wanted to drag her over against him and offer his shoulder as a pillow, but how could he? She'd probably take offense and demand—rightly—that she and April be returned to the airport forthwith because he was not to be trusted.

He unclipped his seat belt and struggled out of one sleeve of his jacket, shaking his hand until it was loose. Reaching over, she helped him pull the other arm free, and he said, "Ball that up and use it as a pillow. Lean against the door and go to sleep."

"Thanks," she said, but before she did, she helped him get his seat belt fastened again, and he nearly groaned aloud at the feel of her hands brushing against his hip.

She folded his jacket neatly, stuffing it between her head and the side window, and leaned on it. "I am getting tired, but I can never sleep in a car."

"We won't be home for an hour, so close your eyes. Even if you can't sleep, you can rest for a while. Just relax and let yourself drift."

"Mmm," she murmured, her eyes sinking shut, a smile on her face. Several minutes later, she said, without opening her eyes, "Will you talk to me? Your voice makes me feel warm inside."

Eric started. Had she said what he thought she'd said? "Excuse me? Are you cold? I could turn up the heat." Even though it was the eighteenth of June, for her he'd turn off the air conditioner and turn up the heat.

Her eyes tired to open, but fluttered closed

again. He had to jerk his attention back to the road
when a super-transport truck gave him a long blast
of an air horn for weaving. "Not cold. I . . . simply
like the sound of your voice."

He let out an explosive breath. For the life of
him, he couldn't come up with one intelligent
thing to say.

"Flying lessons," she murmured. "Tell me about
your first one."

With a bemused sensation clouding his mind,
he found himself doing as she asked, remembering aloud the sweaty-palmed fear, the excitement,
the exultation when the instructor told him he
had control, the thrill of feeling the plane respond
to his command. "There was a sense of freedom
like I'd never known before," he said. "And the day
I soloed, I felt that I'd been re-created somehow,
that the man who'd driven to the airport that
morning was not the one who landed the plane in
the afternoon. When my instructor ordered me
down, I felt as if he were tearing me from the only
environment in which I could really breathe."

A glance at her showed her eyes still closed, her
breathing even; then, slowly, with an almost inau-
dible sigh, she slumped, and he suspected that
she—the woman who "can never sleep in a car"—
was asleep.

"We found him, you know," Sylvia said, startling
Eric as she came awake when he stopped at a
traffic light.

He smiled. She must have been dreaming. "Who
did you find?"

"Googly. My dad called the bus company, and
there he was in the lost and found. We got him

before bedtime that night. He lives on my dresser now."

"I'm glad." It was true. While he hadn't been dwelling on her loss of a favorite teddy bear, he was, he discovered, unexpectedly happy to learn that she hadn't suffered for long.

"Where are we?" Sylvia rubbed her eyes like a sleepy child, then stretched. The childlike aura vanished, to be replaced by that of a sensuous, tawny-gold lioness, and he nearly choked over a different set of emotions.

"Almost home," he said in a voice that didn't quite belong to him, then cleared his throat. "This is Offenburg, near Baden Solingen, where the air base is. We passed the gates a few miles back, while you were sleeping."

Sylvia sat up straighter, indignation making her scowl. "I wasn't sleeping," she said. "I told you, I never sleep in cars. I simply rested my eyes."

He had to smile at her adamancy. "Well, if you weren't sleeping, you sure gave a good imitation of it."

Her eyes widened, spilling golden laughter. "Did I snore?"

He chuckled, a nice warm sound that made her want to slide over and curl up beside him, rest her head on his shoulder. She stayed right where she was, almost clinging to the edge of her seat in her determination.

Could she have been sleeping? Dreaming? They'd been talking about her teddy bear, and then . . . other things. Then he'd given her his jacket, and she'd put her head on it, enjoying the scent of leather, the scent of his after-shave or cologne or maybe just his skin, and she'd known she shouldn't be taking such pleasure in those things, but then he began to wash her with his voice, and it had blended with her . . . dreams, so yes, she guessed she must have slept. How strange.

The light turned green, and Eric eased the car ahead. After bumping over a set of railroad tracks they were on a two-lane highway, going out of town across flat, pine-studded land, following the road as it twisted between hills terraced to the very top with vineyards gilded by the setting sun. He slowed as they drove past a family all riding bicycles, the dad out in front, followed by six children, going down in size like steps, each bike getting smaller, with the rear brought up by a watchful mother who kept her bike several inches closer to the road than that of the youngest child.

Sylvia laughed as she turned to look at them out the rear window. "That's a lovely sight. They all look so happy. Sort of reminds me of *The Sound of Music.* My mom and sisters and I make sure we watch it at least once a year to remind us of how wonderful romance is."

With a woman like Sylvia, Eric thought, romance might be pretty damned wonderful. The thought was so powerful, so compelling, he found himself asking, "Do you ever want what your sisters have, marriage and children of your own?" A woman who loved kids must surely want some, and that would mean marriage.

"Oh, yes," she said eagerly. "Sometimes I want someone of my own so bad I could cry."

She was truly an extraordinary woman, he thought. Most women, when asked that question, shrugged and acted coy, saying something like, "Oh, maybe someday . . ." in order to hide from the guy that she was doing what Sylvia admitted freely, searching for Mr. Right. His voice sounded hoarse as he asked, "Do you have anybody specific in mind?"

She laughed. "Nah, but that's because I'm still enjoying the search. I suppose, like most thirty-year-old women, I give every unmarried man I see the once-over as potential-husband material." She squinted at him, lips pursed, head cocked to one side, making a big production of examining him closely, looking him up and down. "Hmm, not bad. You married, mister?"

"Don't look at me!" His alarm was only half pretense. "Sorry to disappoint you, but I'm married to the air force." *You are, so remember it,* he told himself sternly.

She laughed. "Don't worry. You're safe from my predation. Uniformed men do not turn me on. Don't forget, I was raised by a man in a uniform."

That irked him. "I thought you claimed a very happy childhood."

"I did. I do. But it was rigid to the extreme, and I won't live by the numbers ever again."

She giggled, that sweet, lilting sound he knew he'd never forget, and added, "Boy, did Mom and we kids cut loose when Dad was out on exercise! We ate when we wanted, what we wanted, and where we wanted, even if it was in front of the TV with plates on our laps. We slept late on Sunday and all too often on school days, too, and had to scramble to catch the bus, or Mom would have to drive us. We giggled half the night with friends sleeping over on weekends and went barefoot in the rain."

Eric was quiet for a moment; then, with a frown, he said, "I thought, from what you said earlier, that you loved your dad."

She stared at him. "I do! Heavens, did that sound as if I don't? He's a wonderful father. The discipline was good for us. But so was the relaxing of it when he was away. It was like a vacation, but we were always glad when he came home and we got back into our nice, comfortable routine again."

"So why won't you marry a man in uniform?"

"Now, did I say I wanted to marry anybody?" she challenged with a laugh.

Four

"Is this it?" Sylvia said as Eric pulled into a paved parking area beside a two-story stucco house with a large, darkly painted balcony overhanging the front. "Are we here?"

"We're here."

For a long moment they sat staring at one another, and she thought he might say something more, but in the backseat April awoke and said plaintively, "Grandma?" Eric sighed quietly as he opened the door.

"No, honey-bun, but I'm here." Turning, Sylvia smiled at the sleepy child. "We're at your uncle's house. Did you have a good sleep?"

April nodded and hung on to her doll, shoving the blanket to the seat as she sat erect. Carrying Eric's jacket, Sylvia slid out of the car as he opened her door, and stretched gratefully before reaching back inside to unlock April's door. She turned as light flooded through the front door of the house and a stout woman came bustling down the steps. The woman glanced at Sylvia curiously, and then, cooing and patting, welcomed April volubly and warmly in fractured English, smiling all over her round, rosy face.

April, after a moment's startlement, beamed, listening as if she understood every word.

"This is Frau Fischer, our housekeeper," Eric said presently. "Frau Fischer, this is April's traveling companion, Sylvia Mathieson. She will be staying with us for a few days, until April gets used to being here." The woman frowned in confusion, glanced from Sylvia to Eric, clearly not having understood much of what he said until he spoke in German. Then she smiled, nodded, bobbed a little curtsy, and murmured, *"Guten Abend, Fräulein,"* before she took April's hand and led her up the steps, still chattering away in a patois April clearly found reassuring.

As they entered the house, the phone rang. Eric excused himself and stepped through another doorway, and the ringing stopped. Sylvia followed the sound of April's laughter and entered the kitchen, where the child knelt on a chair watching Frau Fischer cook pancakes on a huge griddle atop a small stove.

"April, it's your uncle," Eric called, and she hopped off her chair, looking around in confusion until Frau Fischer showed her the way into the living room, where Eric waited, the phone in his hand, a smile on his face. Sylvia followed, took the comfortable chair Eric offered her, accepted a glass of white wine, and sat listening to April regale her uncle with exaggerated tales about how the wings had almost fallen off their plane.

Several minutes later, April held the phone out to Sylvia. "He wants to talk to you," she said, and scampered back to the kitchen, clearly finished with her uncle for the evening.

Rob McGee thanked her for coming along with April, then said he meant to heal fast so he could get home in a hurry. "From what Eric tells me, it's worth having a broken leg if it means I get to meet you. He said that you're too pretty to describe, then went on and did so in great detail. I've never met a woman with golden eyes."

Sylvia couldn't prevent her gaze from swinging to Eric's face for a startled instant. She took a large sip of her wine and nearly choked. He'd said that? Well! And she'd thought, because he hadn't lived up to his reputation and tried to put the make on her, that she wasn't his type. Of course, his saying she was pretty didn't necessarily make her his type, but the glow of knowing he thought she was warmed her more than the wine.

She said good-bye with her mind in a whirl as April came back from the kitchen to say that their supper was ready.

An hour later, with the tub filling in the bathroom next to the guest room Frau Fischer had readied for April, the child asked, "Where are you going to sleep, Sylvia?"

"In your uncle's room," Eric answered for Sylvia. "Frau Fischer is getting it ready for her now. It's that one over there, in case you need to find Sylvia in the night." He pointed out a door that stood open across the hall. Then, with a brief touch on Sylvia's hand, he smiled and said quietly, "Come on back downstairs when you get April settled, okay?"

"Sure," she said, and then had to wrench her

attention back to the bathtub before it overflowed. Darn, but it was far too easy to enjoy looking at Eric Lind, even when he was walking away. Hmm. Maybe especially when he was walking away.

It didn't take long to get April bathed and ready for bed, and when she'd been duly tucked in and kissed good night, Sylvia was herself slumping with weariness and happy to let Frau Fischer take up the task of sitting with April until the child fell asleep.

"I didn't take you shopping." Eric said when she came back into the living room and sat on the sofa, shoving back the damp sleeves of her sweater, pulling her daisy-faced watch from the pocket of her jeans and strapping it around her wrist again. She fumbled it, and Eric sat beside her, taking over the task. His fingers felt too large and too awkward but got it done somehow, while his heart thudded heavily at being so close to her, touching her, breathing in her scent. When he finished, he didn't move away from her, but sat there wishing he had an excuse to sit closer. His loins tightened painfully, and his heart nearly stopped when she leaned her head back on the sofa, only inches from his shoulder.

"It's okay," she said. "I can see I won't be needed here, the way Frau Fischer and April have hit it off. I can probably fly back tomorrow."

"Still, I'm sorry," he said. "I said I would, then forgot all about it, and forgot as well that you wanted to jog for three miles."

"Don't worry about it. Maybe Frau Fischer will lend me a nightgown, and I can rinse out these things for morning. As for jogging, I think I can miss one day."

"On you, Frau Fischer's nightgown would look

like a very short, very wide tent. I'll give you one of my shirts to sleep in, instead."

He couldn't resist touching her hair, brushing it off her cheek with the backs of his fingers. It was smooth and soft and much finer than his own coarse hair. "Leave your things in the bathroom, and I'll see they're taken care of. Are you ready for bed now, or would you like a nightcap first?"

She stretched, making fists high above her head. "Mmm, a nightcap, I think. I need to unwind a little. That snooze in the car sort of took the edge off, and if I go to bed too early, I'll be wide awake and starving, with my system demanding caffeine, about three in the morning."

"If you wake up starving anytime, help yourself in the kitchen." He opened the door of a multicompartmented wall unit. "Brandy?" he asked, and when she nodded, poured a pair of drinks into balloon glasses and came back to the sofa, sitting beside her, his long legs stretched out well past her bare feet.

"I'll leave a pot of coffee on the stove ready to go," he offered, handing her the drink. "All you'll have to do is turn it on and let it do its thing. Before you go up, I'll show you where everything else is. Better yet, wake me if you wake up early, and I'll cook you some breakfast. Frau Fischer lives next door and doesn't come in until seven."

She inhaled the fumes and cocked her head to one side. "Thanks, but if I do wake up, I'll take care of myself."

He lifted one brow. "This hotel has twenty-four-hour room service, madam."

Sylvia laughed and ran her thumb and pinky finger through her hair, flipping it back into its cowlicks. "I've heard that one before. Though I must say you don't look like the room-service waiters I've run into in England. They always manage to look disapproving of a guest demanding bacon and eggs and strong black coffee at three o'clock in the morning, even though their hotel advertises twenty-four-hour service. And the time I made the mistake of asking for hash browns . . ." She tilted her head up, looked down her nose, and said in a stuffy, huffy tone, "Madam, 'hash' is not on our menu."

Eric chuckled, and she added, "The concept of fried potatoes in the middle of the night was about as easily understood as that of black coffee before dawn."

She laughed softly and shook her head, then leaned it against the back of the sofa again, as if her muscles were too weary to hold it up. He ached for the right to draw her into the curve of his arm, tuck her head onto his shoulder, and cradle her while she unwound. But hell, if he did, it would take *him* about ten years to unwind. As it was, he didn't anticipate sleeping for a week or two.

He nodded sympathetically. "I've had a few run-ins with British restaurant help myself."

"Have you been to England often?" They asked the question at the same time, and then laughed. "This time," he said, "you are going to go first, and I'm not answering any questions about me."

Sylvia inhaled the pungent brandy fumes again as she warmed the glass in her hands. "I've been three or four times on business."

"Delivering children?"

"No." She sipped. "A few times, it was sensitive documents for a financial firm, things they didn't want to entrust to a courier company that simply sends packages through its system unaccompanied. Another time it was taking a pampered, much-beloved dog over and seeing it into a kennel to start its quarantine."

He crossed one ankle over the opposite knee as he half turned toward her. "Where else have you gone? Anywhere exotic?"

"Not much foreign travel, I'm afraid. Hawaii a time or two, once to Bermuda, and once to the Netherlands. Most of my work is domestic and to the States, because most of what I do is escort the products of broken homes."

"Is that what put you off marriage?"

She looked at him quizzically and sat up straighter. "What gives you the idea that I've been put off marriage?"

"Haven't you? In the car you suggested you were, even though you said you wanted what your sisters have. Is there somebody? Are you engaged?"

"Nope, not me," she said, leaving him with the sudden conviction that her brief, cheerful reply hid pain.

"But you were?"

She sipped again and set her glass down. "Were what?"

"Engaged."

She shrugged. "Sort of. It didn't work out."

"When?"

"A few years ago."

"Are you over it?" he asked, turning his brandy glass around and around in his hands, not looking at it but at her, his eyes intense, his mouth a taut line above his stone-carved chin. Forbidding.

For a moment he thought he saw anger flick across her face, and regretted his impulsive question. "Sorry," he said. "It's none of my business." Dammit, that was the second time he'd had to say that to her. He'd have to learn to keep his thoughts to himself, but something about her tended to bring out the worst in him.

"No apology needed," she said shortly. "I'm completely over it."

"But you're angry."

She managed a smile. "Not at you. At myself. I was stupid and naive, and I don't like to remember that time in my life."

Oh, yes, she'd been angry with herself, ashamed of her totally bad judgment, still got furious when she thought of it, still felt the same deep, never-ending shame and grief. There must, she'd often thought, have been some clues she could have read. But if there had been, she hadn't seen them, blinded as she was by love, and she'd made a complete and utter fool of herself over a man she couldn't have. The result was something she'd have to live with for the rest of her life.

And if she hadn't been forewarned, she'd have been in as much danger of making a fool of herself over Eric Lind, uniform or not, as she had over Dean Edderly. There had been the same instant affinity between her and Dean as she'd felt today with Eric, the same kind of immediate attraction— at least on her part—though the two men weren't even of the same body type or coloring. Eric Lind was hands-down better-looking and . . . She snapped herself off that track quickly.

"You don't look as if you're over it," Eric said, and to her surprise and to the detriment of her equilibrium, reached out to run the knuckle of his first finger down her cheek to her chin. "Does it still hurt you to think about him, Sylvia?"

She jerked her head away under the guise of turning to pick up her brandy glass, and gazed around the room, heart hammering uncomfortably hard in her chest. Why had he touched her like that? Was this the beginning of the big seduction scene? "There's no point in wasting tears on a jerk," she added.

"Were you very much in love with him?"

After a moment she nodded. "Yes. Very much. I . . . wanted to have his babies."

That, to her, characterized her relationship with Dean, but she'd long ago come to realize the emotion might have had something to do with both of her sisters having recently given birth. Three adorable new babies in the family were enough to set any woman's maternal juices flowing.

"And?"

"And . . . we agreed to disagree. I wasn't the woman he . . . needed."

"Because of your work?" She hesitated, and he made a face.

"I'm sorry. I shouldn't be asking you all these questions. But I feel as if we've known each other for . . . a long time, and it seems strange, not knowing everything about you. I think we could be friends, Sylvia."

She smiled at him and didn't argue the point; friends were all they could ever be, and oddly enough, at the moment, that seemed pretty good to her. They talked then of many things—schools they'd attended, summer jobs they'd had, people they knew, even discovering two mutual acquaintances within the military community.

"So, even if it hadn't been for April, we were destined to meet," he said, sounding pleased.

She sat up and took another drink; then, still cradling the glass, she leaned back again, only mildly surprised to discover Eric's arm behind her neck this time. She yawned. "Do you believe in destiny?"

"Sure. At least sometimes. Like horoscopes. I believe in them when they say what I want to hear."

She gave him a quizzical look. "I didn't know guys cared about horoscopes."

He leered. "We learned to when women started asking 'What's your sign?'"

Sylvia laughed around another yawn, and he curved his hand gently around the tip of her shoulder, tilting her toward him. Easily, she swayed that way until the wall of his chest stopped her and she rested there, content. Her brandy sloshed in its glass. She righted it and reached out a limp and languid arm to place it on the table.

She didn't want any more of that. Simply leaning on Eric, feeling his warmth, feeling the strength of his arm around her, hearing the steady thud of his heart under her ear, was as heady as brandy, she thought. She knew there was a reason she shouldn't rest on him like that, but she was so warm and relaxed, she couldn't quite remember why she shouldn't do it.

She nestled closer, turning toward him and sliding an arm over his chest. She closed her eyes and said sleepily, "Nobody asks that question anymore. You talk like a guy who's been out of circulation a long time."

He chuckled. "I'm still out of circulation."

She knew she didn't believe him, and that there was a reason not to, but that, too, escaped her. "Me too," she said as she yawned and tried to lift her head, but Eric held her there, his hand warm and hard on her cheek, slightly rough, his fingers in her hair. She thought about telling him to back off, but it was nice, for a few moments, to pretend . . .

"No you're not," he said. "You told me in the car that you were enjoying the search."

"Maybe I lied. Maybe I don't want anything to do with men. I won't even hire one as a courier. They're simply too much trouble."

Eric chuckled again. "Pretty sexist attitude, Ms. Mathieson."

This time she managed to shake off his hand and open her eyes, lifting her head far enough so she could look up at him through her eyelashes. "Yup. I learned sexist attitudes working with men."

Her eyes fell shut again as she let her head drop back to rest on his shoulder. "Know what?"

As in the car, he was almost overwhelmed by a massive rush of tenderness. She looked like a sleepy child, but when he followed his compulsion to touch her again, to feel her hair against his hand, her skin, like downy satin, on his fingertips as he let them trail down her throat, he knew that she was all woman—and he was all man. "What?"

"I'd hire you."

"You would? Why?"

"Because I like you. I wish we really could be friends."

He drew in an unsteady breath and lifted her face with one hand so he could see into her eyes. The bones of her face felt sharp and delicate in his palm. "Can't we be?"

"Well, no."

"Why not?"

"Because . . . ladies' men scare me."

"Ladies' men?"

"Yeah. You know. Girl in every . . ."—she grinned up at him—". . . airport?"

He laughed softly, derisively. "You think I'm like that?"

She rubbed her cheek against his shirt front. "Aren't you?"

"No, Sylvia."

She sighed. It was nice to pretend to believe him. but . . . "Still, we couldn't conduct a very successful friendship, because you live here, and I live thousands of miles away." And that, she realized suddenly, was the *only* real impediment she saw to their friendship, which was really, really weird, and when she'd had about twelve hours' sleep, she might be able to figure it out. Didn't she care that he was a Don Juan?

"You got here on an airplane once," he said. "Couldn't you come back that way again . . . if a friend asked you to?" Oh, Lord, what was he doing? Asking for trouble was what!

She sighed and shrugged his hands off, picked up her brandy, and sipped a time or two, mulling over his question. "I don't know," she said finally, frowning. "I suppose there's no reason why I couldn't, is there?" She smiled. "Let's be friends, Eric. Good friends. Platonic friends."

He took her glass and set it down, gave her a strange, confused look and a crooked smile, seemed about to ask something, then shrugged. "Okay," he said. "I can live with that. I guess." It was the only kind of relationship he could see for them, but even as he admitted that, he was forced to admit also that it would never be enough.

He leaned back, pulling her with him, stroking her hair, molding his hand over the shape of her head, setting up a response in her that threatened her equilibrium drastically. She tried to breathe evenly, but his scent affected her so much, she found herself hyperventilating. She tried to stop breathing altogether, but that was no improvement. Her head spun and spun and spun, and when he spoke again, his voice sounded hollow and far away.

"Friends should know all about each other, right? Hopes, dreams, plans for the future, past relationships—"

That woke her up. "No!" It was a yelp of dismay. "Not *all* about each other." She sat up quickly and took what a connoisseur would have called an inelegant gulp of her brandy, holding the glass in both hands, staring at him over its rim. She did not want to have to tell him her secrets. She wanted him to go on liking her, respecting her! She set the glass down so unsteadily that it teetered on the edge of the table.

He grabbed it and set it farther back, giving her another of those puzzled looks. She smiled quickly, nervously, and said, "That brandy has gone right to my head. I think I'd better go to bed."

"Except for one gulp and a couple of dainty sips, you've hardly touched it," he said. "It's exhaustion that's gone to your head, not booze, and I shouldn't be keeping you up. I'm being selfish."

"That's okay," she said, then yawned behind her hand. "With a little girl in the house, I suppose your normal . . . uh, lifestyle will have to be curtailed. If we're going to be friends while I'm here, of course I'm happy to keep you company."

"That's very generous of you," he said, his mouth twitching with a suppressed grin. "But I like my company awake."

Now that she'd successfully distracted him from

a subject she preferred not to discuss, she didn't want to go to bed. She wanted to spend as many moments with him as she could, because their time together was so limited. After all, it wasn't every day she made a new friend, especially not one so sexy and warm and who smelled so nice and provided such a tempting pillow for her head. . . .

"I'm awake!" she insisted.

"Sure you are," he said. Gently, with an arm behind her back, he propelled her to her feet. "And you never sleep in cars."

He steered her up the stairs and right to the bathroom door. "I'll bring you a shirt. Don't fall asleep in the tub."

"I'll shower."

Eric waited for her outside the bathroom door, telling himself that was doing so only because she was so tired and he was afraid she might fall. But when she came out, he could only stand there and look at her, his gaze traveling from her bare toes up over her slim calves, her shapely thighs, and her breasts filling out the chest of his shirt in a way that he found as deliciously erotic as he did her damp hair and her scrubbed, shiny face. Over her shoulder she still carried that huge tapestry bag, and he reached out to relieve her of its weight.

"Come on," he said, putting an arm around her again and walking her to the bedroom he'd indicated earlier. A small lamp illuminated the room dimly, and he lifted the covers back for her. "Here, crawl in."

Sylvia giggled. "You're going to tuck me in?"

"Of course." He smiled, wishing she'd giggle more often, but then he remembered the sound of her very husky, very adult laugh, and wanted to hear that again, too, before she slipped away into sleep. How, he wondered, was he going to let her go tomorrow? No. Think positive, he told himself. Think about how you're going to keep her here. He briefly considered sending Frau Fischer on an unexpected vacation. "You tucked April in," he said. "And now it's your turn, so hop in."

Feeling like a ten-year-old and loving it, Sylvia did as he asked. Snuggling against the feather pillow, she lifted heavy lids and met his blue gaze. "Who's going to tuck you in? Frau Fischer?" She laughed at the notion.

He flicked off the lamp, leaving only the light from the hall shining across the foot of the bed. "Don't worry about me," he said. "Window open, or closed?"

She shoved the thick down comforter to her waist. It was warm in the room. "Open, please. I do, you know, worry about you. It's funny, isn't it, but I do." He opened the window and a rose-scented breeze billowed the sheer white lace curtains into the room until he shut the drapes over them. "I worry about your finding yourself trapped into entertaining a strange woman and a little girl instead of the ladies you normally have, uh, have here. Or do you generally go to them?"

She giggled again and hitched herself up on one elbow. Shoving a strand of hair out of her eyes, she turned her head to take in the huge bed, in which she took up very little space. "This is such a big bed, I suppose you probably bring them here."

He stared at her. What was she trying to do? Drive him to drink? "Aren't you forgetting this is Rob's bed, not mine?"

She grinned. "I'm sure yours is no smaller." As he returned to the side of the bed, she reached out and ran a hand up over his forearm to his elbow, tugging until he sat beside her. "Poor Eric. Stuck with a platonic friendship. Listen, if you want to bring somebody home, anytime at all, I promise to keep out of sight. I'd hate to think of such a virile, gorgeous hunk as you suffering needlessly."

Bemused, enchanted, delighted, he had to laugh as he gazed at her. Gently, he eased her back down again on the mattress. She really was out of it. "They tell me suffering's good for the soul."

She frowned. "This next week will probably buy you a trip right into heaven."

He watched her long white fingers as they slid from his elbow to his wrist, feeling them rub over his skin, over the bristles of hair, feeling them viscerally throughout the rest of his body. "It . . . might," he said hoarsely.

The hell it would. If she didn't stop touching him, if she didn't turn those huge golden-brown eyes of hers off, he'd show her platonic!

Quickly, before he could be tempted further, he stuffed her arms under the covers, pulled the comforter up to her chin, and tucked it down around her shoulders. "Good night," he said firmly.

"I can't remember the last time somebody tucked me in," she said, and grinned impishly. "How about a good-night kiss?"

Sweat broke out on his neck and face. "I . . . uh, Sylvia, no. I don't think that's such a good idea."

"Why not? Didn't you say we were friends? I know I don't turn you on, Eric, but that's okay. I don't want a man-woman kiss. Merely a friendly kiss." *Liar, liar, pants on fire* . . . It was as if both her sisters were in the room with her, chanting.

"What do you mean—" His voice cracked and he broke off, cleared his throat in the hope that he could speak normally. The futile hope. "What do you mean, you don't turn me on?" he croaked. "You do. You turn me on so much, I'm going crazy trying to keep my hands off you, and you're not making it any easier, talking like this."

She laughed again, that warm, sultry, *adult* sound that got to him so fast and so strong. He closed his eyes. Lord, it was like a physical touch. "Like what? Like telling you I find you gorgeous and virile, a real hunk?" He opened his eyes again. That *was* a physical touch! She'd worked her arms free of the covers, had propped herself up on one elbow, and had planted one hand smack in the middle of his chest. It burned.

"Don't pay any attention to my saying that," she said. "I didn't mean to embarrass you, but Lord knows you must have heard it hundreds of times before, considering all the women in your life. Of course it's true. You're one of the most attractive men I've ever met, but that doesn't mean I expect you to find me attractive, so you don't have to be kind and pretend. Honestly, Eric, I don't mind that you don't. I'm content with friendship. In fact, friendship would be better for me to share with you because, believe me, if you were mine, there'd be no way I'd willingly share you with anybody, and certainly not with all those other women in your life."

He stared at her, his chin sinking farther and farther as he replayed in his mind what she'd said. One thing stood out above everything else. "You think I'm attractive?"

"Oh, yes. Totally."

Okay, so he was tall, dark, and, some people

said, handsome. Especially in uniform. He wasn't stupid. He knew that. But . . . She'd never seen him in uniform. She didn't even like men in uniform! "You like my . . . looks, huh?"

She nodded. "And your personality. And your voice. Especially your voice. It vibrates"—she smiled as she slid her hand up his chest to his throat, fingertips touching lightly against skin— "right here, when you speak. It's like a thick, rich chocolate syrup, pouring over me, turning me all soft and warm and gooshy inside."

He stared at her, and there was nothing soft and gooshy about the way she made him feel. He was so hard he ached.

"But you don't need me to tell you that," she said. "All those other women must tell you all the time."

"All . . . what other women?"

She dropped her head back down onto her pillow and let her hand fall to lie curled, palm up, beside her face as she grinned at him conspiratorially. "The ones you and Rob . . . entertain here." Patting his hand, she went on, "Hey, it's okay. I'm a woman of the world. I understand the way guys like you and Rob live, and who would I be to disapprove? You're both single, well over the age of consent, and if your commanding officer lets you rent a house instead of living in Bachelor Officers' Quarters, it must mean he trusts your discretion. So it's okay with me. I still want to be your friend."

He turned the lamp back on and studied her face in the shadowy light it cast, looking for signs of mockery, some indication she might be kidding. She was owlishly solemn now, her pupils huge and black, blocking all but a slight rim of golden brown. "Sylvia," he said, meeting those sober eyes, "listen to me. Hear what I'm saying. Rob 'entertains' women, if you insist on using a euphemism. Frequently. I do not. I live pretty much the same here as I would in BOQ. I choose to live off base because I like the privacy of my own home and need an extra room for my computers, but not because I have a steady stream of women in and out."

He drew in a deep breath and let it out quickly before saying, "Now that we have that straight, let me tell you again that you do turn me on." He tightened his hands on her shoulders, feeling the bones and muscles under his fingers as the warmth and scent of her rose, in tandem, to threaten his sanity.

"I do?" There was a half-smile on her lips, but her eyes held a hint of doubt. "You haven't acted, well, interested."

"I haven't? If you think that, then you haven't been paying attention. What did you want, for me to jump you the minute we were alone?"

She laughed, a soft, breathless sound that slid into his bloodstream and made it bubble. "Maybe not what I wanted, but it was what I . . . expected, I guess, and when you didn't, I had to conclude that I'm not your type. It's okay, though. There's nothing wrong with my self-confidence. There are men whose type I am, so—"

"Sylvia." He shut her up by placing a pair of fingers across her lips. "You haven't been listening to me. There is only one thing I want more than to give you a good-night kiss," he went on, "and that is to crawl into that bed with you and give you a thousand kisses, all over your delectable body. Ever since I first saw you at the airport, I've been having fantasies about you, and me, and beds."

Her eyes were wide and searching as she stared at him. "Oh."

"Now," he said softly, bending low over her, still holding her gaze. "Knowing all that, do you still want that good-night kiss?"

She parted her lips slightly. The tip of her tongue came out and wet them. She sucked in a shaky breath and said, "Yes."

As if for punctuation, the breeze blew the door shut with a soft, definitive thud.

Five

A gulp of air jammed tight in Eric's throat. *Yes?*
She'd said yes? He swallowed dryly. He should get
up and walk out of there, leave her to her sleep; he
knew she was punchy with exhaustion, probably
didn't know what she was doing, what she was
saying, but it was as if she had trapped him in the
web of her golden gaze, snared him to the side of
the bed by the enchantment of her laughter, her
smiles, that rough-edged voice that so fascinated
him. By saying yes.

He let her shoulders go, slid his hands down her
body to her waist, began to lift them away, started
to sit up, prepared to leave, and felt her hands
wrap around his wrists.

"We shouldn't do this, you know," he whispered.

"Why not?" Her hands slid from his wrists to his
elbows, fingers soft and strong as she curved them
around his arms, under his rolled shirtsleeves.

Bending ever closer, feeling the softness of her
breath on his cheek, on his lips, he said, "Think
about it."

"It's just a good-night kiss."

Blood pounded heavily in his veins. It thundered behind his ears, making his head feel thick and robbing him of sense. He felt the satin of her lips against his, tasted them with the tip of his tongue. A massive tremor swept over his body as he squeezed his eyes tight shut, fighting for the strength to pull away before it was too late. "Sylvia . . ." he murmured. "Oh, God help me . . ."

Sylvia felt him shudder. It started at his shoulders and passed through his body, making his hard arms vibrate within the circles of her fingers, sending a quiver through the hip she felt pressed against her leg through the thickness of the duvet. His mouth parted gently over hers. Hers trembled open under his. Gently, exploringly, their tongues touched, tasted, retreated. She closed her eyes, savoring the taste of him, wanting more, breathing in his scent, feeling his muscles quiver again as he held himself up from her, so that only their lips touched. It was a brief kiss, a quiet kiss, and when it was over, she felt as if she had been reborn as someone she had never known. Languidly, she opened her eyes and looked at him as he thrust himself back from her. He smiled into her eyes. "Good night, angel," he said.

From a long way away she heard her own voice saying, "Good night." She lay there, floating in a sea of soft feathers, aware of every corpuscle and nerve ending in her body, a red haze obscuring much of her vision. How could such a small kiss have affected her so strongly? Was there some kind of alchemy in his kiss? What would happen if he kissed her again? What would happen if she kissed him the way she wanted to? She let her hands fall from his arms, lifted one, and touched his lower lip with a fingertip. "Good night," she said again.

He didn't move, but continued to sit there, watching her face, one hand cradling her jaw, his eyes dark and unreadable.

Why didn't he go? Why didn't he end this torture? Was he waiting for her to ask him to kiss her again? Did he want her to throw herself at him? No! She wouldn't. She didn't do that! That wasn't her style. It wasn't? Asking for a good-night kiss wasn't throwing herself at him? Telling him he was madly attractive wasn't throwing herself at him? Lamenting his not being turned on by her wasn't throwing herself at him?

Oh, Lord, she didn't care! She had to do it. This was not something she could control. Her arms slid around his neck, hands filtering through his hair as she pulled his head down to hers again. "Once more," she murmured. "Just once."

He groaned. "No. I'm leaving!" Then, gently, he kissed her brow, moved his mouth down her temple, over her cheek, and fluttered little kisses onto her closed eyelids. Soft and warm and gooshy didn't begin to describe things anymore, and she fought the heavy lethargy that wouldn't let her push him away. She had to fight it, had to find the strength to put an end to this rapture because it was . . . wrong?

Eric heard her draw in a long, unsteady breath and felt her hands spread out on his chest. "Good night," she murmured.

"Good night," he muttered as he filled his hand with a mass of her hair, turning her face up to his. For a long, aching moment he looked at her again, breathing deeply, raggedly, until she opened her eyes and they gazed at him, questions in their golden-brown depths, as many as were ricocheting around inside his own mind.

"Oh, Lord, what am I doing?" he groaned again, and kicked off his shoes to lie down on the outside of the feather comforter that covered her to the waist, drawing her into his arms. Then he kissed her like he'd never kissed anyone before. He kissed her the way he'd wanted to kiss her from the moment he saw her, giving it everything he had, plunging deep, exploring, withdrawing to taste her lips tenderly, adoringly, before plunging within again as a prelude to the true exploration he wanted to make of her body, tasting her, drinking her, showing her, proving to her exactly where his feelings lay and that she was at the center of them.

He forgot that he'd first seen her only hours before. She was his, and she doubted that he wanted her. He had to show her that he did, would always want her, had to make certain she never doubted him again. He strained her to him, touched the skin of her long, slender throat, felt her flesh quiver, felt her respond with a rush of heat, cling to him with the same kind of wild, desperate desire that burned in him, a need to be closer, tighter, united until there was nothing separating them at all.

Her hands tangled in his hair, holding him close, then clutched at his shoulders when he dragged his mouth from hers, shoving her shirt aside to kiss the hot skin of her throat, nibble the tendons there, and her clavicle, then the vee where her breasts began as he pushed them together and buried his face in the softness.

As Eric undid one button, then another, blood rushing hot through his veins at the sight of her small, perfect breasts with their dark pink nipples, he bent and touched one with the tip of his tongue. She gasped in pleasure, arching high. He cupped her breast in one hand, exulting as the nipple sprang into his palm, and she whispered his name, a question he answered by bending his head and drawing that hard nub of flesh into his mouth. He shoved the duvet down, past her waist, over her thighs, and then she was helping him kick it to the foot of the bed, tangling her legs with his.

Any residue of sleepiness fled as Sylvia felt his distinct male hardness pressing into her belly, heard the rush of his ragged breathing, smelled the erotic, pungent odor of aroused man. She spoke his name, loving the sound of it. In response he kissed her again, hauling her tightly against his body, moving in a sensuous dance they could no more have stopped than they could have stopped the world turning.

Mine, mine, mine . . . Eric didn't know if he said the words aloud or not, but they echoed in his head, filled his soul. Her resilient strength delighted him, her size fit his perfectly. She was everything he'd ever looked for, even when he'd been unaware of looking. "Sylvia," he whispered, opening his eyes and gazing at her face so near his on the pillow. Slowly, slumberously, her lashes lifted, and she gazed at him in wordless wonder. "Sylvia . . ." he said again, simply because he could, and then began touching her body all over, discovering its warmth and texture and conformation, branding it into his memory.

Sylvia moaned softly as she succumbed to the incomparable pleasure of his palms smoothing down over her bottom, sliding up under the tail of her shirt, and rising over the skin of her back. She shuddered at the feel of his hands on her bare skin. She stroked his face with her fingers, outlining the shape of his cheekbones, trailing a gentle touch around the curve of his jaw; she traced his ear and drew in a quick breath, the sound of his name, when he caressed the back of her right knee, causing her leg to flex, allowing his knee to fall between hers.

She moved against his thigh, her eyes wide and pleading.

In response, Eric clamped his hands on her waist, lifting her atop him, spreading his legs to make a cradle for her, his hardness pressing between her legs. Her tawny brown hair hung down like curtains on either side of her face. He buried his nose in it. "From the moment I saw you, I wanted to do this," he whispered against her throat. "I knew your skin would taste like this, dreamed that you'd respond to me this way. I wanted you from the word go, Sylvia, before I even knew who you were and why you were striding toward me like a beautiful Norse goddess with sunshine in your eyes."

"Oh, thank God," she murmured. "I felt like such a fool for wanting you."

He slid her down his body until he could look into her eyes. "You did? You do? Want me?" He knew she did, but ached to hear her say it.

She didn't hesitate, didn't demur. "Yes," she said, and moved on him, making him gasp with a pleasure that was too close to pain. She looked at him, her golden eyes filled with wonder and longing, and he murmured "angel" as he turned her onto her back and leaned over her, sliding his hands slowly, sensuously, from her thighs to her waist, then up under her breasts, watching her expression change, watching the flush rise from her chest up over her neck and onto her cheeks, where it gave bright sparkle to her eyes.

"I've never wanted anyone like I want you." He dipped his head and took one of her nipples into his mouth, rolling it with his tongue, nipping with his teeth, while he stroked a hard thumb over the other one.

"Eric . . . Eric . . ." Sylvia ached with need as he suckled on her. Her legs scissored, wrapping around his, rasped by the fabric of his trousers, weaving between them as she moved restlessly, seeking relief from the pounding desire at her core, in her blood. He brought his mouth back to hers, and she welcomed it, popping the buttons on his shirt with unsteady fingers, drawing the sides apart and, with a deep shudder of delight, feeling his chest on her breasts for the first time. It was magic, enchantment, pure erotic rapture, the sprinkling of hair down the center of his chest abrading her nipples, and she arched to him, twisting from side to side to capture more and more of the wonderful sensations, knowing that she was experiencing something she had never known before, something new and exciting and unique, and she wanted to make it last forever, but it was moving fast now, like a runaway freight, and there was no holding it back.

"Oh, Lord, woman, what are you doing to me?" he whispered as he glided his hand down over her belly, where her muscles contracted spasmodically, involuntarily, to his touch; then he parted the hair at the apex of her thighs, probing her folds gently, his eyes on her face, waiting, breath held, for her to tell him to stop.

She could say nothing, though she read the question in his eyes, and he let loose a shuddering sigh as he lifted himself over her, his arms rigid, staring down into her flushed face, then dropped lower, kissing her with such yearning tenderness that she sobbed aloud and cradled his head in her hands, kissing him with more love than she'd known her heart could feel.

Then, abruptly, before completion could take its course, he wrenched himself free of her, rolled away, sat on the edge of the bed with his face in his hands, elbows on his splayed knees, shoulders heaving, breath rasping heavily. "No!" he said hoarsely when she placed a hand on his back. "Don't. We have to stop this. Now."

Why? It was all she could do not to ask, but she knew the answer as well as he did, was grateful that he had been the one to make the decision, regardless of how much it hurt. She clenched her teeth and her fists as she turned on her side, facing away from him, muscles aching with the effort of restraining herself, of not pleading for release, not offering the same to him.

Moments later, he turned back to her, gently, soothingly, stroking her arm from shoulder to fingertip, again and again until slowly, so slowly she wondered if it would ever happen, Sylvia felt her tension begin to ease. Her breath was a long, sobbing shudder as she drew it in, let it out. When Eric lay down beside her again and rolled her against him, holding her, rubbing her back, she could only cling to him, wondering if she would ever be the same again.

A lifetime later Sylvia heard him say, "Angel, you have to let me go now."

"Go?"

"Yes." Gently, he took her arm from around his torso and rolled from her side to the opposite side of the bed. "The phone's ringing."

"Oh." She sat up, feeling stunned. "I thought I was still hearing bells."

Eric lifted the phone, listened for a moment or two, frowning; then his gaze flew to Sylvia's face as he said, "Yes. Yes, she's here. Hold on," and passed the phone to her. Then, ducking under the cord, he got to his feet and grabbed his shirt, sliding his arms into it as he headed for the door to give her privacy.

Sylvia took the phone, stared at it for a second, then said, "Yes? Hello? *Jazz?*"

He paused in the doorway when she squealed, and turned in alarm to see her sitting upright, clutching the comforter to her chest, her eyes wide, filled with disbelief as she listened to someone on the other end. Then, "Oh, Jazz, I don't believe it! A boy!" For a moment, as she listened, she sobbed silently, her forehead resting against her fist, then on Eric's shoulder as he sat on the side of the bed and pulled her into his arms.

"A boy," she repeated, lifting her head to treat Eric to a rainbow smile, blinking her eyes so that tears splashed again, some falling on his chest, others on his hands. "Jazz has a newborn son. I'm telling Eric," she said into the phone. "He's my . . . host."

Her gaze clashed with his and their smiles faded, to be replaced with shock and doubt and confusion as they silently acknowledged how close he had come to being far more to her tonight than "host," and she quickly looked away, embarrassment staining her cheeks.

What should he do? Eric wondered, letting his

arms fall from around her, looking at the top of her bent head. Leave? Wait until she was finished with her call, then try to talk to her about what had happened between the two of them? Pretend nothing had happened? Lord above, he'd never before been faced with this kind of situation, and was completely at a loss.

Finally, while he still sat there irresolute, he realized she was crying again, softly, huge tears rolling down her face.

"Not . . . Shane? But Jazz, you have to call him Shane, you prom—" She broke off, and whatever her sister said caused Sylvia to gasp and turn pale, her eyes filling with such pain that Eric had to clench his fists so as not to snatch the phone and demand that she not be hurt this way. Instead, he steadied her with his hands on her shoulders.

"But, Jazz, I may never have a son of my own," she said, and for a moment she could only weep. Then, "All right. Mom? Hi. You shouldn't have asked her to do that. What if I don't get— Oh. Okay. If Dad insisted, who am I to argue?" She sniffed and wiped her face with a corner of the sheet. "Thank you. Thank you all. For understanding, for caring so much."

She listened for several more minutes, speaking now and again, and Eric realized she was talking with other family members. Then, with a tearful, tender laugh, she said, "All right, Jasmine, you've done a good day's—night's—work and deserve your rest, so go to sleep now. Give everyone my love, and kiss little Matt for me. I'll see you in a few days."

She sniffed again and accepted the tissue Eric offered her, refusing to look at him.

He cleared his throat. "I'm . . . sorry you had to

stay with April and couldn't be with your sister tonight."

Sylvia buttoned her shirt again, concentrating hard on the task. "Even if I'd left when I'd intended to, I'd have missed the birth by a long shot." Her voice was tense.

Coming close again, he touched her face, tracing the salty streaks on her cheek. "Sylvia, who is Shane?"

Her shoulders stiffened. "No one!" she said sharply, pulling back from him so swiftly that he recoiled and took several steps away.

"I'm sorry," he said.

A moment later she raised her eyes to his and said, "So am I. I shouldn't have snapped. I . . . don't talk about Shane."

"I mean, I'm sorry for what happened."

"Nothing . . . happened." She drew in a deep breath and let it out slowly. He saw her swallow. She lowered her lids, showing thick, short lashes with golden tips. "And I'm the one who should apologize for what . . . almost did." Her voice trembled as she flicked those lashes up and met his gaze again. "I know it's different for a guy, that most men will take what's offered when it's offered, and of course, so will some women, but . . . well, I've never been like that." She looked down at her linked hands. "I've never offered myself to a stranger."

At once, he was by her side, sitting on the edge of the bed again. He cradled her chin in his palm. "Look at me."

Reluctantly, she met his gaze. "Am I a stranger?" he asked.

Drawing in a deep, jagged breath, she shook her

head. "No." She sounded incredulous, puzzled to find it was true. "No, you're not."

"Good. Because you're not a stranger to me, either." He brushed her hair away from her face and pressed her back against the pillow. "Sylvia, why did you think what you did about me? About lots of women."

"Mrs. Anderson, April's grandma, intimated it. She's quite disapproving of you and Rob. She said, 'Two men, living together the way they do in that house, instead of in Bachelor Officers' Quarters.' She said it was nothing short of indecent, and that of course your 'goings-on' wouldn't be permitted on a military base. She said she wished she didn't have to expose April to 'all that sexual activity,' but she had no choice. Her late son-in-law had made it clear that if April was ever orphaned, while she might be given custody, his brother was to have access."

"I don't know about that. Rob and I are friends, but we don't spend much time talking about family, his or mine. I told you more about myself today than Rob's learned in ten years, and even while I was doing it I was wondering why I wanted you to know. I knew only that I did, that it was important for us to get to know each other as well as possible, as soon as possible."

He smiled crookedly. "I didn't intend for us to know each other that well, that soon. I only kissed you to show you how wrong you were in thinking I wasn't attracted to you. I honestly didn't expect things to escalate like that. I've always been able to maintain control."

She smiled faintly, not happily. "Me too."

He ran his fingers into her hair, spreading it across her pillow. "One of my first thoughts about you was that there was no way I was going to let Rob meet you, ever. He's the one with the reputation. Well deserved, I might add."

"You . . . don't share it?"

Eric shrugged. "Not deservedly, anyway." He shifted uncomfortably.

"I wasn't asking for details," she said, looking away in some embarrassment while she fumbled to pull the cover higher on her chest.

"I know you weren't," said Eric, standing to release the comforter. He snapped off the light, bent down, kissed her cheek, and said, "I want you to know something, Sylvia." His voice sounded disembodied now that she could only see him as a shape in the dimness. "I've never been a man who climbed into bed with every woman who looked willing. I've never gone that far with a stranger either. But once I started kissing you, stopping was the hardest thing I've ever had to do."

Out of the darkness her voice came softly. "Why did you?"

"Because you . . . you're special. You deserve better than . . . me. And because you're searching for Mr. Right."

Through the open window came the sudden, freaky sound of a cat yowling. Sylvia said, "And you're Mr. Wrong."

"What I am," he said softly, reminding her—and himself—of his career, "is *Captain* Wrong."

"I . . . know."

"Good night," he said after a long, tense moment. "We'll talk tomorrow."

"Sylvia, look!" April bounced on the side of Sylvia's bed where Eric had sat what seemed like only moments before. "Look what I've got. Oma Fischer says they're Easter eggs. She's going to cook them for my breakfast and says do you want some too?"

Sylvia rolled over and glanced at the two brown eggs April clutched, one in each hand. As she moved, something slid under her shoulder, and she felt for it, discovering a single white rose on a short stem with all the thorns carefully removed. The breath left her lungs with a whoosh, and she buried her face in the pillow, smelling Eric, and the rose, wondering where he was. He'd brought her a rose! Had he touched her, maybe kissed her, while she slept? Why hadn't she wakened?

"Frau Fischer says to tell you it's nearly nine o'clock," April said, and Sylvia lifted her face from the pillow.

Nine? So much for waking up starved at 3:00 A.M. her first night on the wrong side of the Atlantic. All it took to knock her out cold was a man like Eric Lind.

"Is that my Uncle Robbie's shirt you're wearing?"

"No, it's Mr. Lind's. Is he . . . is he here?"

April shook her head. "No. He got in his car and went away. His uniform's blue. Uncle Robbie's is green. I got a picture."

Of course. So much for his "We'll talk tomorrow." A military man had to report for duty no matter what. The house could have burned to the ground in the middle of the night. A tsunami could have struck. Aliens could have landed in his backyard. A simple kiss between two strangers could have escalated into something much more potent than either participant had expected or anticipated— but a military man put on his uniform and went to work, regardless.

She knew the routine.

"Don't you want to get up?" April asked.

"No. Yes. Sure. In a minute," Sylvia said. What she really wanted to do was lie there and relive every one of those kisses, feel again in memory his hands on her body. Memory? Memory be damned! She wanted the whole sequence repeated for real, in real time, over and over and over. . . .

"You . . . you go and tell Frau Fischer thanks, but I'll eat later. I need some exercise first."

"Exercise? What for?" Clearly, the concept was unfamiliar to April.

Sylvia sat up and shoved her hair out of her eyes. "To keep me healthy," she said aloud. To keep me sane, she said to herself. To channel my libido into something I can handle.

April sulked. "If you don't get up and have breakfast, then Oma Fischer and I can't go to the market. She's gonna take me on her bike, on a little seat that fits right on behind her, and we'll carry stuff in a big basket in front. She showed me, and there's another bike for you if you want to go." The pout turned to a hopeful smile as April tugged at her hand. "Come on, Sylvia, please?"

"Okay, honey-bun, if you insist, I suppose I better get up. I'd hate to keep you and Frau Fischer from the market, but do you think I could have half an hour to get ready?"

"Sure, but hurry, okay?"

"Half an hour."

Still clutching her pair of brown eggs, April danced away.

Sylvia flung her legs over the side of the bed and wiggled her toes in the rag rug before going to open the drapes. It was a beautiful golden day out there, and she would have enjoyed a long run, but while her clothing lay neatly folded and stacked on the dresser, bra and panties on top, her shoes in the corner by the door, they were no good for running. Poking her head into the hall to make sure it was clear, she scooped up her toothbrush case from her purse, darted across and into the bathroom, emerging five minutes later much refreshed. Though she might not be able to run, there was nothing to stop her from putting in twenty minutes of exercise out there on that big, sunlit balcony.

Six

Sylvia's concentration was so total that she didn't hear the door open, wasn't aware that she was no longer alone, and continued the deep leg bends, the sweeping, powerful, seemingly languid arm and body movements that nevertheless took great power and control to execute correctly. Finally, finished with her routine, she stood leaning against the nearly chest-high wall, breathing deeply, steadily, filling her nostrils with the scent of freshly mowed grass, letting her mind slowly return from its exalted state, and her body from its oxygen high.

"Is that some kind of dance?" Eric asked behind her, and she whirled as he spoke.

Her breath caught in her throat at the sight of him, tall and lean and broad-shouldered, incredibly handsome in his sky-colored uniform. He took off his hat and tossed it through the door behind him, his gaze never leaving her face, and all the deep relaxation brought on by her exercise evaporated as her heart pounded hard in her chest and excitement rippled through her veins at the expression in blue eyes made bluer by the color of his jacket.

Hunger filled Eric as he swept his gaze over her, taking in the shirttails skimming midway down her thighs, her bare feet, her still-tousled hair, the pink cheeks on which the flush deepened and spread as he stared at her. For a moment a hint of something he thought might be fear flickered in her eyes, and she looked . . . trapped. Then her lashes dropped like shutters, and she bit her lip, nervously tugging at the shirt to make it cover more of her.

He winced, clenching his hands into fists at his sides in an effort not to reach for her, drag her into his arms, and haul her through the door into his bedroom to finish what they'd started last night.

Oh, Lord! She was embarrassed! Of course she was! Dammit, where was his sensitivity? What was the matter with him, barging out here knowing that she was still dressed only in that shirt? He was the worst kind of fool, because only a fool reaches out and grabs a woman when she's not even capable of coherent thought, and last night she'd been too tired to make a conscious, considered choice.

He cleared his throat and said, "That . . . what you were doing. I wouldn't have watched without your knowing, but you seemed to be so wrapped up in it, I didn't want to interrupt. It looked . . . interesting."

Sylvia felt chilled by the coldness in his face, the aloof, detached tilt of his head as he ran his eyes over her, clearly in disapproval of her state of undress. There he stood in uniform, looking at her as the commanding officer might look at a disobedient recruit. Dammit, didn't he realize she was completely decent as far as anyone looking up at her from street level could see? No, of course not. From his rigid, military point of view she was improperly dressed, and not fit to be seen in public. She suddenly remembered her father's re-action to the "Itty Bitty Titty Club" T-shirt he'd caught her wearing in the mall at the age of twelve. He'd looked then exactly as Eric Lind looked now. Mortified.

She jammed a hand into her hair, shoving it off her face, swallowed hard, and managed to say, "It's ta'i chi."

A flicker of humor lit his eyes for a moment as he said, "Gesundheit," and to her relief, his mouth curved into a warm smile that nearly curled her toes, but when she smiled back and took a step toward him, his face froze again, making him even more forbidding than he'd been yesterday in the airport. And today she felt vulnerable, as she had not then—uncertain, especially when he folded his arms against his chest in what she saw as a protective stance. He was girding himself to fend her off lest she throw herself at him again.

She swallowed the thickness in her throat. "Thank you for the rose," she said.

He nodded, still tense. "You're welcome. It seemed a bit . . . rude not to be here when you got up in a strange house and all that, but I had to go to the air base."

Sylvia heard the strain in his tone, and hated the hard, tight smile that never reached his eyes when he stepped another pace away from her, as if her nearness threatened him.

She managed a cool little smile in response. Far be it from her to risk intimidating a man who seemed to fear she might make unseemly demands on him and his time. "I understand. I didn't expect you to be here, dancing attendance on me."

Eric thought he detected a note of hurt in her tone despite the polite words, and gazed into her clear golden-brown eyes, searching for the truth, for some clue to her innermost feelings. Abruptly, she looked down in renewed embarrassment, flushing again, and he was in no more doubt; it was obvious that last night's passion was something she preferred to put out of her mind. He had to find a way to let her know that he wouldn't jump her like that again, not without a coherent invitation, and that was something he knew he wouldn't get.

After all, she'd been completely up-front with him—she did not take to men who wore uniforms.

"I cleared things with my squadron," he said, and Sylvia met his gaze, but his expression remained guarded, masked by his thick, dark lashes as he squinted against the sun. "I'm free for the rest of the week to, uh, help you take care of April."

"That's good, and speaking of April, I must get dressed. I promised I'd bike to the market with her and Frau Fischer."

"They've already gone."

"They have?" Just like that? She tried to smile, tried to mean her words. "That's good. I guess that shows that April's settling in and won't need me to stay very long." Pain smacked her in the ribs, pain such as she hadn't expected, along with the knowledge that she didn't want to leave, not like this, not with so many questions unanswered, such as why did she respond to Eric Lind as she'd never responded to any other man in her life?

So, Eric thought bleakly, she's already planning her escape. And why shouldn't she? She'd only come to his house because April was afraid, and now she wanted to run because she herself felt that way. Her sudden paling served to support Eric's estimation of her fear.

"I told Frau Fischer I'd see to your breakfast. How long will you need to get ready? Ten minutes? Fifteen?"

"Fifteen," she said.

He nodded briskly, turned in what she recognized as parade-ground perfection, and strode through the door he'd opened, leaving her to go alone through the one that led to Rob's room.

In the shower, she worked up a lather and rubbed it into her skin, then rinsed off, stepped out, and wrapped her hair in a towel, using another to dry her body. If it took longer than normal to dry her face, there was no one but she to know, no one but she to care. When she finally faced Eric, not a trace of her tears remained.

"Frau Fischer doesn't normally work on Sunday or Monday," Eric said as she entered the kitchen to find him sliding poached eggs onto slices of toast on plates decorated with tomatoes. He'd changed into civvies: a bright red shirt and faded jeans, with the most unmilitarily disreputable running shoes she'd ever seen. They were so filthy they could have walked by themselves, so old they deserved a decent burial, and so tattered they threatened to fall off his feet as he walked, his big toes showing through where the rubber caps had peeled up from the tips. She stared at them in disbelief, only lifting her gaze to his when he spoke again.

"And since she worked yesterday," he went on, "I gave her today off. She's spending the afternoon at her daughter's farm and invited April. When April heard there were baby animals there, she begged for permission to go along."

He pulled out a chair for her. "Sit down. I hope

you don't mind, but I okayed it. I know Rob would have done the same thing."

"It's perfectly all right with me," she said, watching his large brown hands as he carried two plates to the table, setting one before her and the other opposite her. "I have no authority over April, and the way it looks, she doesn't need me. Maybe I should go. I heard trains going by this morning. Is the station near? Would you drive me there?"

He glanced at her from where he stood pouring coffee. "Now? You'd leave without saying good-bye to April?" With quick, lithe strides he came and set her coffee down before taking his own place at the table.

Sylvia cut into a slice of bright red tomato with the side of her fork. She looked at him, found his gaze steady on hers, saw a hint of pleading in his eyes. Pleading with her to stay . . . or to go?

"No, I suppose I couldn't leave without saying good-bye. That . . . that wouldn't be fair, would it?"

He smiled faintly. "Not fair at all. She'll be back this evening after dinner, and you can discuss it with her then."

Sylvia ate in silence for several moments. "That will make it pretty late for catching a flight today," she said presently.

His gaze captured hers again, blue and intense. "There's always . . . tomorrow."

She nodded, looking down at her plate, her heart doing tricks in her chest as a direct response to his expression. There had been a challenge in it, and something else she couldn't name, but it made it difficult to breathe because it was the same kind of expression she'd seen there last night just before he kissed her for the first time.

"Or . . . even the next day," he said. "I did promise to show you a castle."

"Yes." She glanced up quickly, smiling. "It's not as if I have to hurry back for Jasmine's sake."

"Right." Eric cleared his throat and continued to hold her gaze as both of them remembered what had gone on before that phone call.

He reached across the small table and took her wrists in his hands. "About last night," he said. "I'd hate to think that what I did is driving you away."

She swallowed hard. "What *we* did, Eric. We were both there, equal participants."

"All right," he agreed, sliding his hands from her wrists to her fingers as he got to his feet and pulled her up, drawing her several inches closer. "I also want you to know that nothing like that will happen again unless you tell me you want it to, because the last thing I want to do is force you into leaving before we have a chance to figure out what this . . . attraction between us is all about.

"Yesterday," he went on, bringing a hand up to cover her mouth before she could speak, "we agreed to be friends. I think jumping the gun like that sort of put friendship out of reach. This has become, much too soon, a different kind of relationship."

Gently, she removed his hand from her lips. "I wouldn't want a relationship that didn't include friendship, Eric."

He was silent for several beats. "Do you want a . . . relationship? With me?"

She met his gaze steadily. "I don't know. But I would like a chance to . . . find out."

He smiled and leaned forward to brush his lips over hers, once, twice, then more slowly, his slightly parted, a third time. "All right. Now, would you like to go shopping for some clothes to tide you over . . . for however long you stay?"

She returned his smile, and nodded.

"Twenty minutes!" Eric said mockingly as he took Sylvia's hand on the way back to the car. "I thought you were the woman who could choose a new wardrobe in twenty minutes. That took what—closer to ninety? Even dashing from store to store, department to department."

"Alone," she said loftily, "I could have done it in twenty. I wasn't the one who insisted I had to try on five different dresses in one store and four pairs of shorts in another when I only intended to buy one of each."

He grinned as he opened her door for her and held it while she got in. "Can I help it if you happen to look so good in shorts that I couldn't decide which pair was best? And you did buy two dresses." He shut her door and went to put her new tote bag, now filled with her purchases, and his two paper bags, over which he was being ridiculously secretive, she thought, in the trunk.

"One sundress," she corrected him when he was behind the wheel, "and one skirt."

"Some skirt," he said, driving out into the light traffic of a Frankfurt street. "Why did you have to choose the one that comes almost to your ankles? I still think you should have bought the red mini."

"The one I bought can be dressed up with high heels and a fancy blouse for evening, or worn plain with a T-shirt and sandals for daytime, and the mini wouldn't go with anything else I have," she said.

"The long skirt certainly will go with everything, with all those wild colors in it."

She suppressed a sigh. He hated her skirt. She wasn't surprised. Her father would hate it too. "When are you going to tell me what you bought?" she asked.

"Soon," he said, and refused to discuss it as they entered the Autobahn and joined the rapid pace, the powerful car humming along, eating up the miles. Instead, he talked of his life in the air force, comparing notes with her from her days as an army brat. They found a lot of experiences in common, and a lot to laugh about together.

Presently, he swung down an exit ramp and onto a secondary road, which they followed for some time through thick forests, then open fields bounded by craggy rocks that were soon transformed into cliffs forming a backdrop for the early summer crops. Turning onto a narrow road that ran between two of those fields, he nosed the car along slowly, as if searching for something. Then, with a smile of triumph, he spotted a small wooden sign and followed its arrow along an even narrower track to a parking area where only three cars sat in dappled sunlight under trees touched with golden light, and a trail that cut upward across a daisy-studded slope to disappear into a forest.

"What are we doing here?" she asked in the silence after sitting for a moment listening to the engine cool and hearing the muted sound of birdsong in the trees as the evergreen-scented breeze wafted through the car's open windows.

"We're going to have lunch," he said. "There's a little spot I know, just off the trail up that way, that's perfect for picnics. Think your new running shoes could do with some exercise?"

"They certainly could," she said eagerly, flinging open her door and jumping from the car. "And so could I. I could also do with some lunch. I'm starving."

"Good," said Eric, smiling as he tossed her the blanket from the backseat and took his two bags from the trunk. With one dangling from his hand, the other perched on his hip, he linked the fingers of his other hand with hers, and after a moment, she wrapped hers around his.

"How in the world did you find a place like this?" she asked as they entered the woods, the cool shade settling over them. "It's hard to believe there are several cities only minutes away by road in any given direction."

"That's what I like about this place. I was on a *Volksmarch* along this path earlier in the year. There was a refreshment stand set up in the spot we're headed for, and I thought at the time it would make a great place for a picnic with a special lady. This," he added softly, "is the first time I've come back."

Something in her thrilled at the notion, but all she said was, "What's a *Volksmarch*?"

"It's a community hike, very popular in this country. Some of them are ten kilometers, others twenty, even thirty or more. And at the end of each, there's a medal or a plaque for every registered participant."

"Do you do a lot of *Volksmarch*ing?" she asked, thinking of him with a chestful of medals. He had enough chest to carry a truckload.

He nodded. "Nearly every weekend, this time of year." As they continued to walk along hand in hand, two men and a woman coming down the trail toward them stepped aside to make room, the men doffling dark green Tyrolean hats, the woman smiling, then went on their way, laughing and talking.

"Are they on a *Volksmarch*?" Sylvia asked, turning to look over her shoulder at the others.

"No. Just out enjoying the weather. If it were a *Volksmarch*, there'd be hundreds of people on the trail, and we'd have a very unprivate picnic. Not," he added, "that there's such a thing as a very private picnic in a country as small as this, where so many people enjoy the outdoors. Someone's always certain to come along."

When, a mile along the trail, Eric stopped in a sunny glade with a grassy floor and a crystalline stream bubbling past, only a few feet from the side of the path, Sylvia decided it was probably just as well they couldn't count on privacy. It was a pretty place, perfect for lovers, she thought, with a swift reminder that they were not lovers but two strangers seeing if they could become good friends, and then maybe, who knows . . . ?

Eric set the bags beside a moss-covered log while he took the blanket she'd carried from the car and spread it on the grass.

"You sit there," he said, indicating the blanket, "and I'll get this picnic ready."

"What can I do to help?" she asked, feeling useless when he quickly took the bags he'd brought from her, refusing to let her open them.

"Not a thing," he said. "Sit down and relax. It's all under control."

"I'll say!" Sylvia laughed as he shook out a brand-new tablecloth from one bag, spread it on the grass near the blanket, set out a stack of napkins, then added two knives and a pair of crystal wineglasses from the same bag. From the other bag he then withdrew a feast of rolls, cold cuts, a fancy bottle of mustard, and wine, along with a basket of fat, lush strawberries. After opening the wine, he filled a glass and handed it to her, and she leaned back against the trunk of a fallen tree to sip and enjoy.

"Pretty fancy picnic, Captain," she said, selecting a fat, ripe berry from the basket he passed her. He sat beside her, drawing one knee up and leaning his arm on it as he half turned to face her. "Where I come from," she said, "It's a six-pack and peanut-butter sandwiches for a spur-of-the-moment feast in the forest. When did you find time to collect all this?"

"While you were buying those things you wouldn't let me help choose," he said, and chuckled when color flared in her face.

She gulped down the last of her strawberry and took a quick sip of wine. "I guess you think that's pretty silly, don't you? I mean, considering last night . . ."

He touched her warm cheek with his knuckles. "I thought we'd agreed that while last night was wonderful, it came at the wrong place in our relationship. You were right to want to buy your . . . private things in privacy.

"But for now," he went on, "let's let things happen more . . . leisurely, Sylvia."

He set his glass on the log behind him and bent forward. "Like this."

His kiss was long and slow and . . . leisurely, she thought, but it still stirred her to her very depths. They didn't touch each other except for clinging mouths, tangling tongues, mingling breaths, and, when he pulled back half an inch, locked gazes. His eyes were deeply blue as emotion rose and roiled within him, and Sylvia lifted a hand, touched his lips with her fingers, then traced a line around his neck to bury her hand in the thick hair at his nape while he pressed tiny kisses on her cheeks, her closed lids, her ears and throat.

"Eric . . ." she breathed, wanting his lips on hers again, but he smiled, brushed another feathering touch over her cheek, and sat back, dislodging her hand.

"Lunch," he said firmly, and split a roll, stacked a variety of sliced meats inside, added a generous smear of mustard, and handed it to her along with a paper napkin.

"Mmm, good," Sylvia said moments later, swallowing the last bite of her sandwich. "This was a great idea."

"I know," he said smugly. "Because if we were in a restaurant, I couldn't do this." He leaned over, placed a hand behind her head, and pulled her face to his. "Mustard," he said, touching the corner of her lips with his tongue. "And a bread crumb." That was on her chin, and then his mouth was on hers, and she tilted her head back, closing her eyes as she absorbed the sweetness of his kiss, felt it heat her to her core, felt her blood begin to simmer. Then it was over, and he was sitting back from her long before she'd had enough.

He smiled into her dazed eyes. "Another sandwich? More wine? Strawberries?"

How could he think of food? She shook her head. Her glass was still half-full.

"Then . . . how about a *wind beutel*?"

It was difficult to speak. "What's that?" she asked huskily.

He opened a white cardboard box he'd tucked behind the log, reached in, and lifted out a pastry. It sat high and round on his hand, lightly dusted with powdered sugar and spilling whipped cream out an opening near the top. As he passed it to her, Sylvia took the pastry in both hands, staring at it. "That's the biggest cream puff I have ever seen!"

"That is a *wind beutel*, manna from heaven," he said. "Try it. It's name translates as wind pouch, but believe me, the 'wind' inside it is delicious."

"Where do I start?" she asked, turning the confection around and around, looking for the best line of attack.

"Anyplace," he said, taking another confection from the box and biting into it while cream oozed out around the corners of his mouth. He grinned, licked his lips, and swallowed. "There's no neat way to eat a *wind beutel*."

With a delighted laugh, Sylvia opened her mouth as wide as she could and took a healthy bite, squirting thick whipped cream out the sides, wallowing in exquisite flavors, richness that exploded on her tongue, sweetness that filled her nostrils as the powdered sugar rose in a cloud around her face. "Mmm, wonderful," she murmured, closing her eyes to savor the taste and texture and aroma. Licking the corners of her lips and taking another bite, she leaned back and enjoyed the well-named pastry, with its light, flaky shell and filling so frothy it was like eating deliciously flavored air. When she was finished, she opened her eyes and found Eric watching her, fascinated, desire blatantly inscribed across his face, his own cream puff still perched on his hand, in danger of falling to the grass as he paid it no heed at all.

"Lord," he muttered, bending close and running the tip of his tongue over her creamy lips. But when she parted her mouth for his kiss, he lifted his head and said softly, "Watching you eat a *wind beutel* has got to rank among the world's most sensuous experiences, and shouldn't be enjoyed this close to a public path. However . . ." He grinned and held his pastry out to her, minus only one bite, saying, "Here. Eat this one too. Please."

At his importuning, Sylvia giggled, filling him with a different but no less potent delight, and shook her head. "No thanks. The 'wind' inside that pouch probably has more calories than an entire Third World village gets in a week."

He wrapped a hand around her wrist, with plenty of room to spare. "You don't count calories, do you?"

"No, but enough's enough, and I didn't get my customary run this morning." She leapt to her feet and ran to the sparkling stream, where she washed her face and hands.

"Do you really want to run?" he asked, joining her when he'd finished his pastry. He splashed water across his sticky mouth, depriving her of a pleasure she'd anticipated. "I could find a side road and drive along beside you if you want."

"What? You won't run with me?"

He gave her long legs, snugly encased by her new, midcalf-length green slacks, a speculative look. "I have a feeling you'd humiliate me if we ran together."

Sylvia frowned as she got to her feet. "Are you serious? Would it humiliate you if I could outrun you?"

Laughing, Eric steered her back to their blanket, where they began gathering up their picnic remains. "No. Of course not. There's nothing wrong with my self-confidence, either, Sylvia. If there are things you can do better, good for you. There are undoubtedly things I can do better than you."

Linking her fingers with his as they headed back down the trail to the car, she smiled her relief and hopped a few paces as she stuck her foot out in front of her to admire her new running shoes. "With these, I could probably run all the way to your house." Then, with a laugh, she added, "Of course, if I did, they'd end up looking like those disgusting running shoes you had on this morning."

"What disgusting running shoes?"

She stared at him. "The ones you had on this morning. You know, the ones where your big toes hang out when you walk."

He was clearly offended. "There's nothing wrong with those shoes. They have plenty of wear left in them. And they're . . . comfortable. I like them." His hawklike glare challenged her. "You found them objectionable?"

"Oh, no, not at all," she assured him, then changed the subject quickly. "Do you think that shoe salesman has recovered yet from your shunting him aside and personally making sure that my sneakers and sandals fit?"

"I don't care about him," Eric said with a sudden and intense ferocity that startled her. "I care about you, and I didn't like the way he wrapped his hand around your ankle. There was no need for it."

"Except, he was trying shoes on me. Shoe salesmen do that all the time."

His eyes blazed. "Obviously, I'm in the wrong trade."

"I agree," she said. "These fit perfectly, even though you paid little attention to that aspect of things." She grinned. "What, exactly, did you say to him to make him stomp off like that into the back room?"

Eric laughed. "I'll never tell. This way, you'll always need me around to get rid of shoe salesmen when their hands get too friendly with your legs."

Always? With a heavy heart she told herself that his meaning hadn't been literal, but she wished way down deep that it were, in spite of his wearing a uniform and being the kind of man she'd sworn never to link her life with.

All she said, though, was, "I was impressed. You never raised your voice, but you managed to sound really, really angry."

"I was really, really angry. Good guard dogs don't bark, you know," he added solemnly, but with humor in his eyes, "they simply attack in silence."

"How about that," she said with a cheeky grin. "My own personal pit bull. Maybe I should take you home with me, and you could teach my cat a few manners. He has a bad habit of pawing my ankles with his claws out when I don't get the can of cat food open as quickly as he likes."

He stowed their paraphernalia in the trunk, then picked a buttercup and held it under her chin. "You have a cat?" He hadn't seen her as anywhere near that domestic. "What do you do with him when you go away?"

"I take him to my parents' home. He loves it there. There's a big yard full of butterflies and hummingbirds—none of which he can catch, but he never quits trying—and indoors, an aquarium of tropical fish he can torment without getting wet, as well as my dad to irritate." She laughed. "You see, cats don't live by the numbers and can't be 'properly trained.' That cat drives my dad up the wall because he's never happier than when he's got everything flipping or flapping in a stir. But if he ever caught anything, I think he'd die of sheer fright."

Eric thought he might die of sheer bliss, comparing the golden glow the buttercup gave to her skin with the golden glow in her laughing eyes. He twirled the flower across her cheek and under her ear, then down her jaw to her chin and up over her parted lips. She spluttered and tried to push the flower away when she got a mouthful of buttercup pollen, but he laughed and tickled her throat with it, kissing the pollen off her lower lip and then trying to thread the flower's stem into the button-holes at the neck of her green-sprigged cotton blouse. As she helped him, somehow their fingers got tangled up together, then their arms, and for another brief, tantalizing moment, their lips and tongues, but they broke apart to lean against the car like proper, staid picnickers when another group of people came down the trail and past. Eric smiled and greeted the newcomers with the ut-most politeness, as if he hadn't been caught in a passionate clinch, but once they were out of sight, he lifted Sylvia off her feet and whirled her around and around, laughing.

It was the nicest sound Sylvia had ever heard, and something cut loose inside her, winging its way to the sky.

Seven

"What's your cat's name?" he asked when they were back on the highway.

"Froggie," she said.

"Froggie?" He hooted derisively. "What kind of name is that for a cat?"

"An appropriate one for him," she said huffily. "By the time he was six months old, he could spring right onto the kitchen counter from the center of the room, especially if I opened a can of tuna."

"Six months? What did you call him before he learned to play leapfrog?"

"Kitty," she said, in exactly the same tone in which she'd said "Teddy" yesterday, and Eric burst out laughing as they drove from deep shade into brilliant sun and Sylvia fumbled in her bag for her sunglasses.

"What's so funny?" she demanded, perching them on her nose. "My family had a dog that we called Puppy for fourteen years. Most of our cats were never called anything but Kitty, except for Herman and Melissa, and we didn't name them until our next-door neighbors, the original Herman and Melissa, who fought all the time like our two tomcats, got posted."

"You named a tomcat Melissa?" Eric asked, slowing behind a tractor drawing a cart laden with several pigs that poked their snouts out of the slats at the back.

"Why not?" Sylvia looked at him. "We had a girl guppy named Thomas, for Thomas D'Arcy McGee."

"How old was she when she got the name?" he asked.

"I'm not sure, but she'd just had one hundred and three babies all at one time—" At his skeptical look, she said, "Honest. My . . . we counted them. And we figured that must make her a mother of guppy confederation, so we named her after a Father of Confederation, there not having been any mothers of it."

Eric laughed and reached over to curl his hand around the back of her neck. "You are one extremely intriguing woman, Ms. Mathieson."

"Nah," she said. "Not me. I'm as ordinary as they come."

"Ordinary? I'm beginning to suspect you're probably very, very complex."

She laughed as she brushed her hands down over the front of her blouse and tugged her slacks straight. "Sorry. No hidden depths here. What you see is what you get."

He knew, looking at her, that he could never see enough, never get enough, no matter how long he lived. He lifted her glasses off her nose and stuffed them into his shirt pocket, clamping his hand over it as she unhooked her seat belt, slid over to where he sat, and tried to take them back, laughing as he held her off.

"No," he said. "If the sun's in your eyes, pull

down the visor, but don't hide your eyes from me. Do you know how beautiful they are?"

"Eric . . ." Her laughter faded, replaced by an expression that snatched his breath away. "My eyes are a very ordinary brown."

"Your eyes are full of golden sunlight and are the most beautiful feature in a face composed of nothing but beauty."

She stared at him for several seconds, then shook her head, looking almost tearful. "I said it before, and I'll have to say it again, even at the risk of making you blush like you did yesterday. You, sir, are a very sweet man."

He flung back his head and laughed. Lord, it was hard to believe it had only been yesterday they'd met. "I remember your saying that," he said, pulling her close to his side and holding her with one arm. "I don't remember being embarrassed. My feelings at the time were closer to shame."

"Shame?" She tilted her head back to look at him, her silky hair brushing his neck. "I thought you believed I was coming on to you, and you blushed because you didn't know how to tell me I wasn't your type."

"I was ashamed because the thoughts I'd been thinking, about what I wanted to do to you, were so far from 'sweet,' I felt like an utter heel when you said that."

"Oh, really?" She looked at him questioningly. "And what thoughts might those have been, Captain Lind?"

"Never mind," he said with a grin. "They don't exactly come under the heading of friendly 'getting-to-know-you' stuff." He sighed as a couple of cars passed them, then said, "Do up your seat belt, okay? In case you haven't noticed, that tractor pulled off half a mile back, and we're still doing ten miles an hour."

Maybe the car was only doing ten miles an hour, but when she tried to slide across to the other side of the seat, and he held her where she was, saying, "There's a belt where you're sitting," her heart did at least ninety.

As they entered the house that evening after a day spent exploring the surrounding countryside, as well as each other's personalties, they heard April's voice saying "He's not here, Uncle Robbie. He and Sylvia have gone someplace, I think maybe shopping, because she doesn't have any clothes and even had to sleep in Mr. Lind's shirt last night. She slept in your bed, you know, and there was a rose on her pillow this morning, and, oh! Here they are now. *Sylvia!*" The last word was a shriek of delight as April dropped the phone to the desk and shot across the room into Sylvia's arms.

"I had so much fun today! Where were you for so long? I wanted to tell you."

Eric strode forward and picked up the phone, saying, "Hi, Rob. How's it going?"

April bubbled with delight. "I got to ride a donkey today. Did you know that a donkey's called an *esel*?" April quickly recited all the other German words she'd learned, and added proudly, "Oma Fischer says I'll be speaking German like I was born here if I keep on learning as fast as I am. Tante Gertrude—that's Oma Fischer's daughter—has a dog who had puppies, and guess what? She gave one to Oma, and I get to look after it while I'm here. He's—"

There came a series of loud yips from the hallway, followed by the sound of Frau Fischer scolding. Then a small black creature hurtled through the door and flung itself at Eric's legs, growling and snapping, grabbing a mouthful of fabric and tugging as if it intended to drag him from the room. Frau Fischer came to a halt in the doorway, clearly at a loss, and stood gaping as Eric tried to shake off the little dog without hurting it and still maintain his end of the telephone conversation.

"I don't know what's going on!" he bellowed into the phone over the puppy's snarls and April's loud attempts to remove it. "There's a little black rat attacking me, and . . . holy Hannah, it's piddling on my shoe!"

"He's not a rat!" April yelled indignantly over the dog's noise. "He's a little baby puppy, and he's teething, so he likes to chew!" She grabbed the pup around his fat tummy and tugged, while Eric shouted at her to stop squeezing him so hard because she was making him pee more. Finally, April succeeded in breaking him free from Eric's pants. Before she could lift him, though, he wriggled free and grabbed the tassels on Eric's left shoe, hanging on tenaciously, growling all the while as he shook his head back and forth, clearly in the belief that he could vanquish Eric if he only shook hard enough.

"You quit laughing, McGee! This is all your fault, and . . . If laughter promotes healing, then I'll expect you on your way home tomorrow morning at the latest! I . . . oh, holy—" He broke off, looking across the room at Sylvia. "Do you have anything more to say? Anything constructive, that is? No? Then talk to your niece again. I have a hysterical houseguest to strangle."

But Frau Fischer had come quietly into the room and collected both April and the puppy and whisked them back to the kitchen while Sylvia was sprawled on the couch laughing helplessly.

Eric stood glaring at her until she forced herself into sobriety, but when he held his wet shoe up to let the puppy piddle run off it, she was gone again, clutching her middle, tears streaming down her face.

He had liked her giggle. He had thought there wasn't a prettier sound. He'd been turned on by her sexy, husky, grown-up laugh and ached to hear it again. But this one, this deep, uninhibited, right-from-her-toes roar, was the most infectious laugh he had ever heard, and within moments he had collapsed beside her, roaring himself.

"Stop," she begged, holding her middle. "My stomach hurts." But he couldn't. Each time he looked at her, he was off again, and whenever she managed to sober up for a few seconds, she'd glance at his shoe and howl with mirth.

At last, though, it tapered off, leaving both of them limp and exhausted. "Oooh," Sylvia moaned, prodding her abdominal muscles. "I needed that. It's been too long since I've had that kind of a laugh."

He managed to sit up and untie his shoes, kicking them off and setting them aside as he peeled off both his socks, the dry one as well as the wet one. "I have never had that kind of a laugh."

Sylvia stared at him, hiccuped once or twice, and said, "Never?"

He shook his head.

"That's sad," she said, leaning back and closing her eyes, drawing in a tremulous breath and hiccuping again. "That's really, really sad." She giggled.

Eric wiggled his bare toes, studying them, thinking how ugly they were. "Why?"

She opened her eyes and leaned forward, her elbows on her knees, her hair curtaining her face, hiding it from him. He reached out and tucked it behind her ear. "Because . . . everybody needs to laugh like that now and then," she said. "At least once a year, preferably more often."

"Do you?"

She lifted her head and shook her hair back. "Oh, yes. Often. Sometimes Jazz and I set each other off, but mostly, it's my dad and me. We have the same sense of the ridiculous."

Eric experienced a terrible kind of envy, almost jealousy, he thought, and a longing for that close a relationship with someone.

Then, completely out of the blue, Sylvia astounded him by saying, "I like your toes. They're very masculine."

"Huh?" He stared at her, then at his toes, and at her again. "You do? They are? How can toes be masculine?"

"I don't know. But yours are."

Before the topic of toes could be discussed further, Frau Fischer came into the room with many apologies and a spray bottle and a wad of old cloths, seeking permission to clean up after the puppy. Eric nodded absently. Knowing Sylvia liked his toes warmed him right to his . . . well, his toes, he thought, glad no one could read his mind. It was a terribly confused mind right now.

"If you'll excuse me," Sylvia said, gathering up her belongings, "I'll go put these away."

Eric rose swiftly. "I'll come and help," he offered with a slow smile that spoke of things he wanted to do for her when they were in a room with a closed door to protect them.

"No!" Her reply was swift and sharp, startling both of them with its speed and its fervency, with its almost panicky defensiveness. Sylvia shook her head and tried to explain, but her heart hammered so hard in her chest that she couldn't get out another word, just looked at him warily as he followed her into the hallway.

"Hey," he said, and backed her up against the wall, standing with one hand on either side of her shoulders as he looked into her eyes. "All I meant to do is clear out a couple of Rob's drawers for you and make sure there are enough hangers in the closet. I know we agreed to let our relationship grow in a more natural manner, Sylvia, and I'm not trying to push you. Okay?"

Swallowing hard, she nodded and whispered "Okay," knowing that unless she was very, very careful, it wouldn't take much of a push. A gentle nudge would suffice, and a bedroom with a locked door. . . .

"But will you deny me this once in a while?" he asked, brushing his lips over the corner of her mouth. Before she could refuse or accept, April, with the puppy in her arms, came out of the kitchen, calling Sylvia's name.

"Where you going?" April asked, seeing the tote as Eric stepped back quickly, and Sylvia thought she heard a hint of apprehension in the girl's voice.

Good, she thought. I am needed here, after all. That made her feel better, as if April's need somehow justified her staying, proved that it wasn't purely self-interest keeping her here. Then her innate honesty came to haunt her as she asked herself, Oh yeah? Who are you trying to kid?

"I'm only going to put my new clothes away," she said, mounting the stairs. "Come and help me and tell me more about your day, and we'll make plans for tomorrow."

• • •

"Are . . . you . . . sure this is . . . good for . . . a person's . . . body?" Eric puffed as he ran beside Sylvia along a trail through a park he'd driven her to. "Wait. I need a break." He stood, head hanging, hands on his knees, shoulders heaving. "Lord, I haven't run this far or this fast since old man MacAdams caught Kenny Merrick and me in his strawberry patch."

Sylvia laughed. She'd never have thought of Eric Lind as a strawberry thief. "Of course it's good for you," she said, breathing steadily as she ran in place. Her chest rose and fell easily within her royal-blue tank top, her legs moved like oiled pistons below the cuffs of her white short-shorts. "And I think you're faking." In fact, she was sure of it. "You can't convince me that military people aren't required to stay in shape."

"Oh, we are," he said. "But there's . . . shape, and . . . shape." He was glad it was a cool, cloudy morning with a threat of rain in the air. While he wasn't faking, he had been exaggerating a little, but he didn't think he could have done this in the heat.

"Okay," he said after a few minutes. "Let's go." They covered another quarter-mile, and he exerted himself to put on a slight burst of speed as they came to what looked like an adult-size set of monkey bars. It was the sixth such apparatus they'd encountered, the other fitness stations having been different but equally challenging, from rings to tiltboards. Eric welcomed the break in the relentless pace Sylvia had set for their run.

Reaching up to grasp one of the bars, he chinned himself three times, then did a hand-

over-hand maneuver around the set, Sylvia following him. "This makes for a great workout!" she
said, dropping lightly to her feet.

"You didn't chin yourself," he said.

"And, you may have noticed, I didn't use the
rings either," she said. "Women don't have the
right muscles for that. Nevertheless, I can do it."
She proved it by chinning herself a couple of
times, then jogging onward, more slowly now,
beginning her cool-down. "But I prefer not to," she
added. "I like to stay sleek, not develop bulging
biceps and big shoulders."

He turned and ran backward, admiring her.
"You're sleek, angel."

"And you have big shoulders."

He grinned, slowing to a walk and flexing his
arms like a bodybuilder. "And bulging biceps?"

Sylvia laughed. "Show-off." But she could have
spent the rest of the morning simply admiring his
arms and shoulders, to say nothing of his flat
waist and narrow hips. Of course, the ugly, baggy
government-issue gym shorts had to go, but apart
from that, he was truly wonderful to look at.

Noticing her completely unsubtle scrutiny, he
flexed his arms again and leered at her. "Wanna
squeeze 'em?"

"Ohh, yes, please!" she simpered, pretending to
have to stand on tiptoe to reach his arms. She
squeezed, fluttered her lashes, and swooned. Eric
caught her, lifting her off her feet and carrying her
to the side of the trail, where he put one foot up on
a fence rail, rested her against his thigh, and
kissed her until her swoon was almost for real.

She opened her eyes as he set her on her feet,
staggered a little, with only some exaggeration, her
hand to her heart, sighing loudly. "My hero!"

"Don't lay it on too thick," he laughed, "or I won't believe you mean it."

"Mean it?" she said, putting her foot up on the rail beside his, stretching her leg out and bending forward over it, her fingers curling under her instep. Glancing at him sideways from under her hair as she switched legs, she said, "Of course I mean it! How else can I make up for 'humiliating' you by outrunning you?"

"Hah!" he said, standing erect and placing his hands in the small of his back while he stretched his waist. "You haven't outrun me yet, and we're still a ways from the car. You ready to go?"

"All ready," she said, taking off her sweatband and using it to dry her neck before stuffing it into the pocket of her shorts. "Whew! Are you sure you're going to let me in your car before I have a shower?"

"I'll let you in if you'll let me in," he said, wondering what the chances were of their sharing a shower when they got home. His heart rate accelerated even before he started to run.

"Wait," Sylvia said. "We walk back to the car, hero, not run. I wouldn't want to do you in before breakfast."

"Lord," he said with a groan, glad to slow his pace. "Don't remind me. I can't believe that this *is* before breakfast. I feel as if I've been up for hours."

"Uh-oh," she said sometime later when thunder rumbled somewhere off to the west. "I think we might get that shower before we get into the car after all." The parking lot was visible, but still a long way off.

"Nah," he said. "That's just for—" He broke off as fat raindrops began splattering off the hard cinder track.

"You were saying?" she asked.

"Effect," Eric finished lamely, and the deluge

began in earnest while lightning flashed all over the sky and thunder rumbled like several freight trains colliding. "Run!" he shouted, taking her hand, and together they ran along the path, out from under the sparse trees, along a slick, cobbled path, across a grassy picnic area, hurdling the rail fences on both sides of it, and entering the parking lot. But even before they'd reached the grassy place, both had been soaked to the skin.

Never had Sylvia seen such rain outside the tropics. It streamed from the sky, bounced back up from the tarmac, soaking everything in seconds. It ran from their hair, plastered their clothes to their bodies, and the chill wind that accompanied it felt more like November than June, sending blinding curtains of rain slicing sideways as they stumbled onward, between rows of cars, darting around doors that other people flung open as they hurled themselves into shelter. In a violent crash of thunder and a brilliant slash of lightning, Eric brought their headlong flight to a halt at the side of his car.

His keys! Dammit, they were in his pocket, but could he get his shaking hand into the wet, clinging fabric? It seemed to take forever, and Sylvia crouched beside him, trying to hide from the wind and the rain and the . . . Holy hell, now it was hailing, huge, brutal chunks of ice that pelted them like shattered golf balls. Eric's hand got stuck in his wet pocket for a minute, but he managed to get his keys out, unlock her door, and whip it open for her before he bolted around and snatched his open as she leaned across to unlock it.

"Wow!" she shouted, wrapping her arms around herself, shivering hard, laughing in delight. "What a gully-washer! Where did it blow up from?"

"We get lots of summer storms like this!" he yelled back as another rumbling, rolling growl of thunder came at them, ending in an enormous, deafening clap right overhead with a simultaneous flash of lightning that made Sylvia laugh harder.

"Isn't it wonderful?" she shouted over the racket, and he wrapped his hands around her wet, shivering arms, rubbing them lightly, laughing with her, captured by the wild excitement in her glowing face. "It makes me want to get out there and dance like a pagan in the rain!" she said.

He gripped her arm with one hand in case she might try it, and wiped her dripping hair off her face with the other. She laughed and tilted her head back as another bolt of lightning split the sky, flashing in huge zigzags he saw clearly imprinted on her eyes. "Don't you dare," he said. "You look so much the part of the pagan goddess that you'd probably act like a lightning rod simply by the force of your personality!"

She ran a hand into his hair, shoving it off his forehead. "Do you think so? I hope so. I think I am a pagan at heart. I love storms. They're wonderfully exciting and elemental, but to be prosaic, I'm freezing to death. Let's get home."

"In this?" He let go of her long enough to start the engine, then turned on the heater and the wipers, the latter to show her that even at their highest speed they didn't provide enough visibility for safe driving. He shut them off and, reaching into the backseat, grabbed the blanket and wrapped it around her, pulling it right up over her head like a hooded cape.

Sylvia saw the goose bumps on his arms and legs. "You're cold too," she said, pulling one side of the blanket free and grinning at him from within its folds. "Join me," she said. "We can keep each other warm."

Eight

Eric didn't need a second invitation. "This is the best idea you've had all day." he said, drawing the thick blanket over his back. The heater still blew cool, moist air over his dripping legs and feet. Sylvia had kicked off her shoes and shed her socks and was curled in a tight ball, her back against his chest.

"The day is young," she said, her teeth chattering, "and I haven't had much time to come up with ideas, but I'm glad you approve of this one." She squirmed around until she faced him.

Approve? That didn't quite cover it. He liked it so much he was having great difficulty remembering that he was cold. She wrapped her arms around his waist under the blanket and clung to him, shivering, her hair sending little trickles of water down his right arm. He set her back from him long enough to whip off his T-shirt and wring it out as best he could, then used it to absorb some of the moisture from her hair, and his. He pulled her tightly against him, rubbing her cold, wet back through her cold, wet tank top, feeling her hard nipples jutting into his chest, and sucking in a shuddering breath of ecstasy.

The sensation of their upper bodies coming together sent delicious shock waves through Sylvia, and she drew in an unsteady breath, burying her face in the crook of his neck, knowing he had to be as aware of the hardness of her nipples as she was, of the hammering of her heart. To his credit, he gave no sign that the intimacy of this embrace had any effect on him at all as he continued to rub her back briskly, then her leg, and finally her arm and shoulder, with the scratchy wool of the blanket.

Oh, Lord! Eric groaned silently as he rubbed her skin. This was too much! It was more than any man should be expected to bear. "Turn . . . turn around," he ordered. "Let me do your other side."

Obediently, she twisted on the seat until her back was to him again, and he pulled her between his thighs as he scrubbed at her other arm and leg until the skin glowed. But her bottom pressing intimately against him did terrible things to his self-control. He lifted her, then slid under her so that his back was against the passenger door and she was crouched on the seat facing him. This way, he could warm her left side without her sitting on his lap, but it was no better, no easier, because now he could see her face, her half-shuttered eyes, her parted lips. With a soft moan, he pulled her back into his arms, and she enfolded him with the blanket.

Sylvia shivered partly with delight, partly with cold, as she snuggled against him, into his warmth, drew in the scent of his skin and—for just a moment, so quickly she was sure he'd never notice—let her tongue dart over his throat for a tiny taste of him, the salt, the musk, the man. . . . A sob of need shook her, and she hoped it was disguised as another shiver of cold. That one taste wasn't enough, not nearly enough, and she parted her lips again, flicking with her tongue, fighting down an almost overwhelming urge to nip him with her teeth, then kiss the sting better, make him aware that she was going mad with need. Drawing in a deep, tremulous breath filled with the scent of him, she felt herself grow dizzy with the emotions crowding together within her, seeking outlets, threatening to spill over, and held him more tightly, her palms flat against his back, moving slowly up and down, as his moved over her back.

But . . . the touch he gave wasn't the one she craved. How could he be so unaffected by this when it was making her crazy? She wanted to rail against the stern self-discipline that kept him under such rigid control when she suddenly felt his heart hammering hard under her ear, telling her he wasn't as calm and unaffected as he pretended to be. She wanted him to touch her the way a man touched a woman, wanted to know everything he felt, wanted to show him what she felt, to share with him the wild, burning need growing so rapidly inside her.

Don't be a jerk, Sylvia! she told herself. He was acting the way she should expect him to act, for heaven's sake—the way she should want him to act—because they were in a car in a public place, and while no one could see them, the risk of discovery was there. Was it that risk, along with the violence of the storm raging outside, that made this other storm rage within her? But dammit, if he could control himself, then she could do the same!

She sighed and felt his hand come up to cup the back of her head, holding her face against his neck. He stroked her hair, his fingers working through it to her nape, where he touched and massaged and feathered light caresses. Oh, Lord, what was he doing? Did he know that her nape was one of her most sensitive areas, like the back of her right knee?

His fingertips on the top of her spine made shivers and spirals of arousal gather at the base of it. She shifted in his hold, and his chest rubbed against her nipples, hardening them again, making her breasts ache, her belly clench, her insides melt. As another clap of thunder shook the car, she felt his arms tighten, his hand grow bolder as it skimmed past the side of her breast, lingering for a moment before moving on to stroke the skin under her ear.

"Eric . . ." she groaned, trying to lift her head, wanting to tell him he'd better let her go, but the thought was overwhelmed by the burning deep inside for more than this—for his mouth, his body, his hands to move over her with a different purpose, for him to go rigid with this same terrible hunger that built and built inexorably inside her now, seemingly with no end. She ran her lips over his shoulder, pressed her mouth to his neck and said his name again, her yearning throbbing in her voice.

"Hush," he said. "Stay still." He forced himself to leave off stroking the silky skin of her neck, to flatten his palm over her back again, to stop thinking about all the other parts of her he wanted to touch. Just concentrate on rubbing her back, warming her skin. Forget the rest of it, he told himself over and over. Ignore the heat, think about cold things, think about snow, think about ice . . . ice-cream cones, firm round shapes, his tongue sliding over creamy smoothness. . . . Her softness, the hardness of a nipple, the sweet moisture of her mouth parted against his throat, the feel of her darting tongue on his skin . . .

Oh, Lord, stop! The pain of need coiled inside him, twisting his gut, hardening him so much it was impossible to ignore. The feel of her breath shuddering against his throat nearly tipped him over the edge of reason, and he sucked in a harsh, steadying gulp of air as he forced himself to remember that his task was only to warm her, but the heat rose between them, the steam on the windows enclosing them in a secluded world, the blanket cocooning them together, and he tilted her face up. Looking into her eyes, he saw there the same kind of hunger that raged through him, and reached for it, only to encounter her fingertips against his lips.

"I think . . . I think you'd better let me go now," she said, her voice small and nearly lost within the folds of the blanket, under the sound of his rasping breath.

"I . . . can't," he said hoarsely. "Let me hold you like this. Just for another moment. But . . . stay still, angel. Please." Trembling, he rested his forehead against hers, closed his eyes and breathed deeply, raggedly, his hands slowly sculpting the shape of her back, then spreading, encircling her waist under her tank top, his thumbs rising up over the bottoms of her ribs to stroke the curving undersides of her breasts through the satin of her bra. He heard her sharp intake of breath, her shuddering release of it, and leaned his head back to look at her as the blanket fell away.

Her lips were parted, her eyes half-shut, her cheeks flushed, and her nipples upstanding, taut. "Eric?" she said, her voice shaking, and he groaned as he pressed her face to his chest, holding her tightly there. He must not! He must not! But, oh, God how he wanted this woman!

The moment went on and on, and within Sylvia tension coiled and grew, spiraling higher and higher, tighter and tighter, until her trembling was no longer even partly from cold, but entirely from need. She grew hot and wet inside, melting, yearning for his hardness, and she thought she would explode if she couldn't tilt her head back and kiss him, part her lips and take him deep inside her mouth, open her legs and take him deep inside her body. She moved against him, shifting restlessly, the agony building. There had never been a need like this, never such intensity of desire. She opened her mouth, pressed it to his throat again, and felt as much as heard his deep groan of protest, but instead of stopping he tangled his hand in her hair, drew her face up, and lowered his mouth onto hers. She took him in eagerly, crying out softly, and then was silent except for a deep, thankful sigh.

Taking his hand, she drew it to her breast, moving within the cup of his palm, wild with need, sobbing softly now, then purring her delight as he took his mouth from hers and drew her nipple deep inside his heat and wetness.

It wasn't enough! With a groan of frustration, he snatched her shirt off over her head, popped the snap on her bra and pulled it down her arms, flung it away, sat gazing at her beautiful, hard breasts, the nipples pointing at him with cheeky insistence. He groaned again, bending to pull one of the hard buds into his mouth again, this time without the interference of clothing.

Sylvia cried out with the sweetness of the soft tugging and ran her nails down the center of his back, around his waist, lower, skimming over the fabric of his shorts, brushing the stiff hair of his thighs as she arched back to give him access to her other breast.

He gasped his pleasure at her touch, caught her hand, pressed it to his rigid tumescence, and thrust his hips forward as her palm curved to accept the shape of him.

He slid a hand over her belly, his fingers curving in to run around the legs of her shorts, seeking her heat, pressing upward in a blatantly carnal search, rubbing back and forth over the wet cloth, driving her wild as he continued to stroke her breasts with his tongue and suck each nipple in turn until she ached so badly inside she knew she could take no more.

"Eric . . . Eric . . . please," she begged, easing herself out of his mouth, lifting his head to look into his eyes. They were dark with emotion in his flushed face; his hard lips invited her, and she drew his head to hers, opening for the thrust of his tongue, tangling hers with it as she lay back . . . and lost him. The cool, hard plastic of the steering wheel slid past her shoulder, then her back met the soft leather of the seat, and Eric levered himself between her legs, shifting with her, still seeking her mouth, moving over her, muttering curses when the wheel got in his way as he twisted sideways.

He ached for release, fighting the constraints of

the enclosed space, his shorts and hers, seeking the haven of softness he knew he would find between her thighs. His hands gripped her knees and slid upward, then he exulted in the silk of her skin as he ran his palms up the insides of her thighs, past the juncture at the top and over the slight rise of her abdomen, feeling for the tab of her zipper, fumbling for the button at her waist, his fingers thick and clumsy in their haste. Her lips parted in her glowing face, and she whispered his name over and over as he tried once more to reach her, to lock their mouths together even as he wanted to lock their bodies together.

In frustration, he tried to crowd past the steering wheel, and his elbow hit the horn button with a loud and shocking blare of sound that jerked him back to reality.

"What?" Sylvia said. Lifting her head, she opened her eyes, rising up on her elbows, blinking in the brightness of the sun on the steam-covered window, staring at him as he stared back at her, gulping in huge breaths of air, letting them out in tearing sighs. "Eric? What was that? I . . . oh . . ." She groaned softly and lay back, covered her mouth with one hand, her breasts with the other, as sanity returned.

"Oh, Lord," Eric said, his face taut, his mouth a hard, pale line. His chest and shoulders heaved as if he'd been running, and his legs trembled as he knelt there, leaning over her, one hand on the wheel, the other on the back of the seat. His upper arms quivered with tension. "The . . . sun's out," he said numbly.

She could do nothing but nod and lift her shaking hand from her mouth to wipe her hair out of her eyes.

He thrust himself back from her and sat leaning against the passenger door, his eyes shut, his breath slowly coming under control. "Oh, God," he said finally. "I'm sorry! I didn't mean for that to happen." He lifted his hips off the blanket and tossed the end of it to her.

Sylvia struggled to a sitting position behind the wheel, glad that steam still covered the windows. "Me neither."

Didn't you? Didn't you? she demanded of herself, loathing herself. She squeezed her eyes shut again, only opening them when he drove one fist into the other palm, castigating himself.

"I let myself forget where we were, Sylvia, how . . . public this place is, and dammit, I wasn't even considering protection. Hell, that was the most irresponsible thing I've ever done, and I can't apologize enough."

"No. Don't. You don't have to apologize." Sylvia picked up her bra from under the wheel and looked at it with distaste, then dropped it again. They'd tracked grit into the car, and the garment was filthy from its time on the floor. Finding her tank top on the dash, she donned it, grimacing as she did so, pulling it away from her body as much as she could.

For several moments there was silence in the car; then, with a soft sigh, Sylvia reached over and switched the heater to defog. The windshield began to clear, and the side windows let streams of sunlight in near the tops.

She opened the door of the car to get out.

"No," Eric said. "Stay where you are." He flicked the keys hanging in the ignition. "You drive home."

She lifted her brows and shoved her damp hair

back where it clung to one cheek. "Really? Drive your precious Alfa?"

"Really, drive my 'precious Alfa,'" he said mockingly. He smiled grimly. "It will hurt me less to see you do that than to see you getting out of this car looking the way you do and giving every man in the area a wet-T-shirt treat. Drive, Sylvia."

But when she faced the front, she didn't put the car in gear, only sat there looking more and more miserable, her lower lip jutting a bit, her brows drawn together.

"What's wrong?" he asked, running a hand down her sleek shoulder and arm. "It's simply that you look so well kissed, so . . . beautiful, that I don't want to . . . share you."

She flinched away from his touch as if he had hit her. "It's not that. I . . . I have something to say, and I'm trying to find the right words, words that won't make me either sound slutty and cheap, or give you the impression I have a highly inflated idea of my own . . . sex appeal."

She turned and faced him. "What happened, Eric—I mean what almost happened—wasn't your fault. I started the fire, I'm the one who fanned the flames, and I'm the one who let it get out of control." She bit her lip and added quietly, "And I did it on purpose. Started it, that is, not let it get out of control. I wanted to . . . to see if I could make you lose it because . . . I don't know why, exactly. Maybe it hurt my ego for you to hold me nearly naked in your arms and not respond. I wanted to shake your gentlemanly, military cool. And when I did, when you responded, I didn't want to make it stop because it—" She paused, wet her lips, and swallowed. "Because, well, it felt too good."

For an instant, she closed her eyes as she drew in a deep breath, and then she went on, her open, honest, unhappy gaze never faltering. "I'm sorry for and deeply ashamed of what I did. I think I did it because I knew I could trust you not to . . . let it go too far. Not here, not in a parking lot in broad daylight."

He ran a hand through his hair as he stared at her; then, after what seemed like an eternity, he smiled slowly, ruefully. "Can I make a suggestion here, please?" She nodded, and he went on. "Don't . . . don't trust me too far, angel, okay? Because that felt pretty damn good to me too."

"Okay," she whispered, staring at her hands where they gripped the wheel.

"And, Sylvia?" She looked at him. "It wasn't all your fault either. You told me storms excite you. I wanted that excitement. I went . . . looking for it."

She smiled after a moment. "I guess you found it."

Suddenly, he laughed. He grinned wolfishly, clearly pleased with what he'd found. "I guess I did. There's a certain . . . magic that happens when we kiss. It's very, very easy to get carried away. But we already knew that, didn't we?"

Sylvia nodded. "My mother used to tell us about that kind of feeling."

"What did she tell you about it?"

She smiled. "When we were young, she said to beware of it, and not to let ourselves get into situations where getting carried away was possible. In other words, no parking on deserted roads at night."

Eric laughed softly. "What did she say about well-used parking lots in the daytime?"

"If she'd known there was a man like you in the world, she'd have warned me about them too." She paused, a ghost of a smile hovering in her eyes. "When I was young."

"And now that you're not a teenager?" he asked. "What would she say about us . . . today? And the other night?"

Sylvia laughed then, that husky, sexy adult laugh of hers, and it was all he could do not to haul her back into his arms.

"About today? She'd tell me I should have shown better sense."

His eyes were intensely blue as they bored into hers. "And the other night?"

She hesitated only a second before saying, "My mom's a strong believer in reaching out to grasp the moment, especially if it's . . . right."

He rubbed the pad of one thumb over her bottom lip. "I'd like . . . very much . . . for it to be right for us all the time, Sylvia."

Again, she nodded. "I would too." She could easily visualize a life that included this man and an eternity of loving. Loving? Yes! It hit her then, that love was what made it so right for her to be with him. Only, how could she be in love with him so soon? It was all she could do to take a deep enough breath to say, "But . . . it's only been two days."

Long enough for me, he wanted to say, only he couldn't. There were too many things in the way, too many things he hadn't sorted out in his own mind, and there was still her dislike of his uniform and all it stood for. What it stood for was what held him back, too, because he had sworn never to drag a woman into the kind of life he'd chosen for himself. It wouldn't be right. It wouldn't be fair.

"Three days," he said. "We met on Monday." He held up one finger. "We spent Tuesday together." Another finger popped up. "And this is Wednesday." Finger number three went up.

They searched each other's eyes between his three fingers for several moments, and he looked away first, dropping his hand to his lap and turning to face the front. There were no answers. Not yet, and he knew as well as she did that his day count wouldn't hold even a single raindrop if examined too closely.

"Shall we go?" he asked. "April will be waiting for her trip to the air base. Or was it the Stuttgart Zoo today?"

"Base this morning, and you said something about paddleboats at Heidelberg this afternoon. Then it's the zoo tomorrow, and Europa Park the next day," Sylvia replied. Then, tentatively, "Are you . . . are you sure you want to do all this stuff? I could rent a car. Major McGee did say he'd reimburse me for any added expenses."

He looked at her again, smiling faintly. "Are you going to be in all those places?"

She nodded and slid the car into gear.

Eric's hand covered hers on the steering wheel. "Then I want to be there too."

"You knew that was going to happen!" Sylvia spluttered, and wiped her dripping face with her arm as the boat came to a halt in the calm pool it had splashed down into after a wild ride along a track with too many quick right angles, then a stomach-wrenching dive down a watery chute.

Eric laughed heartily as he handed April out of the boat to the waiting attendant, then stood himself to help Sylvia out. "Of course I did. Why do you think I made you ride in front of me?" Under the guise of drying her face with his handkerchief, he bent and whispered in her ear, "Did you think it had anything to do with wanting your delectable little bottom tucked up against my . . . against me?"

She huffed and said, "Of course not," though that was exactly what she'd thought, and she'd very much enjoyed that aspect of it, too, as well as having his arms wrapped tightly around her waist. "April didn't get wet." She took the child's hand. "Lucky for you you're a shorty, kid, and could hide behind the windshield."

April asked eagerly, "Can we go again, Mr. Lind? And this time, I want to sit in the middle so I can get wet and look like Sylvia."

Eric looked at the damp top of Sylvia's sundress and grinned. "It'll be a few years yet before you can get wet and look like Sylvia."

"For a man who was so desperate to hide my wet T-shirt from the world the other day that he let me drive his precious Alfa, you're pretty free and easy about it now."

"Now," he said, taking her other hand, "you at least have something under that dress besides . . . woman."

The way his eyes ran over her breasts had a salutary effect on her nipples, and they rose to the occasion like trained seals, she thought in half-amused dismay. He lifted his brows. "Or do you?"

Sylvia laughed softly and watched his eyes darken. "That," she said, "is for me to know and you to . . . wonder about."

He caught her around the waist with one hand as she whirled past him, and hauled her back to his side. "If I remember that phrase correctly, it ends differently."

"Not when I say it, it doesn't."

"We'll see," he said. "We'll see," and Sylvia suddenly found herself wishing they weren't in the middle of a crowded amusement park with a little girl in tow.

Wednesday, Thursday, Friday . . . she thought, mentally counting the days they'd had together, days of laughter, of fun, of sneaking kisses behind April's back, holding hands and sharing ice-cream cones and telling glances. And the evenings, when the kisses didn't have to be sneaked but could be enjoyed to the utmost—or almost to the utmost, along with good conversation, more laughter, and sometimes small flares of temper when they disagreed.

She knew he suffered as much as she did from wanting more than they knew they should take, and slept as poorly, because when she emerged onto the balcony for her morning's t'ai chi routine, he would be there, fully dressed in his atrocious exercise gear, to watch her. Then, as soon as Frau Fischer made her appearance, long before April was up, they'd go to the park and run together. Those early-morning periods were the only time they could be completely alone.

Tomorrow, though, she thought, feeling giddy at the prospect, April was to spend the day with Frau Fischer's family again, and she and Eric could be alone.

"That was a sad-sounding sigh, Ms. Mathieson," Eric said, sliding an arm around her as they turned down the path toward the exit from the park.

She shook her head rather than give in to the

impulse to rest it on his shoulder. "Not sad, just tired," she said. "It's been a long day."

He grinned. "Never mind. You can sleep all the way home."

For once, she didn't bother to protest that she never slept in cars. In Eric's car, she did.

She wasn't asleep, though, as they left the Autobahn on Saturday morning and swept along a woodsy road with steep cliffs on either side and only occasional breaks where more distant hills could be seen on the far side of the valley. When, at a break in the cliffs, Sylvia saw through the branches of the sycamore trees a granite edifice high on the top of a hill, she sat forward.

"Oh!" she exclaimed. "Is that our castle?"

"That's it."

"It's beautiful," she said. "April was wrong to choose the farm today. I think she'd love this. It looks like something out of a fairy tale."

"It does, doesn't it?" he murmured, glad beyond measure that the two of them were alone today, wishing the castle were really as ethereal as it looked with the wisps of morning mist still clinging to its ramparts, wishing it were far, far away, on a sunlit hill above a secret valley where nobody but the two of them could go. Apart from simply visiting castles, she had him building them— castles in Spain, castles in the air, cloud castles, silly, insubstantial things that he knew would blow away in a puff of wind, and as deeply as he longed to, he didn't dare start relying on them to do anything else. But as he met her open, happy gaze, his heart lifted to soar among the clouds, and he smiled into her eyes.

"Schloss Birkenhorn," he said, slowing to enter a narrow blacktop track that disappeared abruptly thirty feet beyond around an outcropping of granite. Sylvia gripped the sides of her seat as the car's nose tilted up at an acute angle, blocking her vision of the road ahead.

"Are we going up this?"

He nodded, concentrating on the road. "It's the only way up."

"What happens if somebody comes down?" she asked tautly, and nearly moaned aloud at his reply.

"Both of us move over."

"Move over where?" With a sick feeling in her stomach, she glanced at the sheer drop on her side of the car and found herself edging away from it. Terror flooded through her, tightening her throat, threatening to close it off as the memory of another road, another steep flank, rose up.

"Let's hope nobody comes," she said, striving for lightness, trying to force herself to be calm so as not to distract Eric as she knew she might have distracted Shane that terrible night, by yelling at him to slow down. But she sucked in a sharp breath as another car poked its nose cautiously around the corner ahead and Eric moved over—toward the edge.

Sylvia leaned to the left, dizzy, all her effort concentrated on trying not to cry out while she heard the wheels going off the pavement with a small thud, heard the sharp splatter of roadside gravel bouncing up under the car for what seemed an eternity. Then, miraculously, the other car was gone, and the road was all theirs again. With difficulty, she let out her breath and drew in another, another, another—too fast, she knew, but unable to control herself as the drop on her side grew longer and longer, the slope more and more precipitous.

Up and up they went, the road circling the small mountain, the sheer fall from level to level drawing her eyes as she stared at it in fascinated horror. When a massive tour bus appeared around the bend ahead, she knew she was about to die and held her breath, waiting, fighting against it because now, with Eric in her life, she wanted more than ever to live. With a soft moan she closed her eyes, fists clenched in her lap, sweat beading her upper lip, and her heart racing madly in her chest as she girded herself for the initial lurch, the shriek of metal against stone, the crash of breaking trees, and the oblivion that had been denied her last time. . . .

Nine

"Sylvia . . . Sylvia!" Eric's sharp tone as much as his warm hands on her wrists brought her eyes open, and she stared at him, slowly becoming aware of her surroundings, realizing the engine was stopped, the car was pulled well off the road—mercifully away from the edge and her door was open. Eric crouched outside the car beside her seat, his eyes dark with concern.

Sylvia breathed. They had not gone over the edge, and the road was twenty feet away on her right with another tour bus grinding its slow, ponderous way down.

She swallowed, hoping to coax moisture into her dry mouth and throat. "Hi," she said inanely, trying to smile. "Where's the castle?" She desperately wanted to dab the moisture off her forehead and lip, but Eric's hands still gripped her wrists as he stared questioningly into her eyes.

"Up there," he said with a jerk of his head. "Around another half a dozen or so bends. Are you all right?" He shifted his fingers around her left wrist. "Your pulse is about to hit Mach one."

"Don't be silly," she said. "I'm fine." It was hardly a lie at all. Despite his opinion, her heart rate was beginning to decline toward more normal levels, and she could breathe again. "If the castle's there, why are we here?"

He lifted her hands from her lap, held them on his palms, and watched the tremor in them for a moment before he tucked them into the warmth of his neck, holding them there. "What is it, angel?" he asked softly. "Heights? If it is, we'll turn around and go back down right now. I won't subject you to the view from the top of a castle if you're afraid of heights."

She shook her head and rubbed the lower part of her face on one shoulder, then took a hand back from his clasp and wiped her forehead under the pretext of pushing her hair off her brow. "Not heights," she said, and smiled. "Just . . . edges."

"Edges?" He studied her. "You love speed, but hate roads with . . . edges?" Didn't she know how dangerous the one was, and how really innocuous the other?

She nodded, feeling sick again as she glanced at the road over Eric's shoulder as if expecting it to have crept closer while she recovered. "Isn't it silly?"

"No, of course it's not." He knew most phobias had no root in reason. "Why didn't you tell me at the very beginning how scared you were?" he asked, suddenly sounding and looking furiously angry with her. "There were two or three places low down where I could have turned around."

She gave him a ghost of a smile, keeping her eyes on his face, never even glancing at the edge looming so large in her mind. "Because I really thought I could handle it." She frowned. "I *was* handling it, wasn't I? I don't remember making a sound. Why did you stop here, so near the top?"

"You were handling it," he said. "I stopped because *I* couldn't handle what was happening to you, once I realized you were afraid." With a sound something like a moan, he pulled her out of the car, then stood swaying back and forth as he held her tightly in his arms. "It was awful, seeing you like that, so silent, and so terrified. I don't ever want to see you like that again. We're going back. I promise you, the trip down will be easier; our lane hugs the hill all the way."

"No," she said, flinging her head back. "It's not far now, is it? I refuse to have come this far only to go back like a coward, Eric."

He admired her for this display of courage as much as he hated himself for having got her into this situation. "Not far at all," he said reluctantly, reading her firm determination in her eyes. If she really wanted to go on spite of her fears, the best thing to do, he knew, was get it over with as quickly as he could—but he still needed to hold her. He slid his hands around her back, pressing her close, swallowing hard. He needed, desperately, to tell her . . . something that was forcing its way up, choking his throat, making his head spin. He strained her closer. "Sylvia, I . . ." he began, and then his voice died in his throat. He stared at her, his mouth moving, no sound coming out.

"What is it?"

He wanted to say it, could feel it building within himself, but how could mere words be enough to cover it? Whatever this was, it was huge, all-encompassing, and he didn't know where it had come from so suddenly, or even what it was, but it was there. She gazed at him, questioning, and the sun slanted through the branches above them to spangle her face with gold and her hair with sparks of light, and to give her eyes, with their thousand unanswerable questions, an ethereal glow.

"I . . . I . . ." He couldn't go on, could only draw her even more tightly into his embrace, pressing her to him from thigh to breast while he kissed her hard and swiftly, prodding her mouth open with his tongue, thrusting deep inside. He could feel her instant response in the ragged catch of her breath, the softening of her in his arms, the immediate hardening of her breasts on his chest. When he lifted his head only a moment later, they were both breathing as hard as if they'd run all the way up from the highway far below.

"I don't know what to do," he said, gripping her shoulders, shaking her back and forth, not hard, but for emphasis. "I'm falling in love with you, Sylvia! I've been falling in love with you since the day in the airport, but I didn't recognize it because I don't—didn't—believe in love at first sight. Every time I touch you, or see you, or think about you, it gets worse, but I didn't know what it was until I saw you so scared and knew I had to keep you from being like that ever again. Keep you safe. Secure. Protected."

She blinked, her mouth curving into the happiest, most radiant smile he'd ever seen, an Olympic-gold smile, a buried-treasure-found smile, a million-dollar-lottery-win smile. "You are?" she asked incredulously. "In love with me?"

Oh, holy hell! She liked the idea! "Yes, dammit!" he all but bellowed, giving her another small shake.

Sylvia stared. This was the strangest declaration of love she'd ever heard! He glared at her as if it were all her fault, and she didn't know what to say because it so clearly distressed him. He clamped a hand to the back of her head and kissed her again, just as hard and even more briefly, then set his forehead against hers, rocking it back and forth. "Oh, Lord, I don't know how to stop it." He made a sound that might have been a laugh. "You have to help me here! How do I make it go away?"

Her laugh could have been a sob as she clung to him. "I don't know, Eric, because I have the same problem." The only difference was, she knew of several things she wanted to do about the "problem," and stopping it wasn't one of them.

He looked into her eyes, not really believing her, bemused, his hands trembling on her waist. "You do?"

She nodded. "So, if you ever find out how to make it go away, let me know, okay?"

"Yeah," he said, his tone suggesting that she shouldn't hold her breath waiting. "Sure. I . . . Lord! Sylvia, are you certain you feel the way I do?" How could she, and still look so . . . sane?

Leaning into him, she brushed her mouth over his, running the tip of her tongue along his lower lip, feeling it quiver in response. "What's 'certain' got to do with anything?" she asked. "Either love is, or it isn't. If it wasn't, we wouldn't feel like this. If it is, we don't have to ask about certainty or uncertainty. We simply . . . know."

Under her hands, she felt his chest still rising and falling rapidly, his heart hammering hard. His eyes gazed into hers with . . . with what she could only think was . . . uncertainty. "Does what you said make sense to you?" he asked.

Sylvia considered, then laughed. "Of course not. I'm in love, Eric. Nothing has to make sense today."

"It doesn't?"

She shook her head and slid her hands around his neck. "No. Hasn't this ever happened to you before?"

He gazed at her for a moment, then kissed her again, finally lifting his head because he was feeling decidedly dizzy. He realized that all the blood had left his head and rushed south as it always did when he kissed her. That was enough to make any man dizzy. "Funny, huh? But . . . never." He held her closer, and saw by the laughing, delighted surprise in her eyes that she knew where all his blood had gone, too, and didn't mind in the least. Could she really want a man with no blood in his brains?

Her eyes told him she did.

He swallowed hard. "I . . . love you, angel," he said raggedly, then threw back his head and looked up into the trees as he felt hot moisture sting his eyes. He had to take several deep breaths before he could look at her again, and when he did, he saw sparkling tears standing on her lashes. He caught one on his fingertip, tasted her salt, and kissed the rest away.

"I love you!" he said again, laughing out loud. "Ah, damn, but it feels good to say that to you, Sylvia! I've never said it before, to anybody."

"I love you, Eric," she said, more tears beading on her lashes, catching the sun, making rainbows in her eyes. This time, he didn't try to hide the stinging heat in his, but blinked rapidly until it went away, trying to laugh at himself but ridiculously embarrassed nevertheless. Grown men didn't cry for happiness!

"And I've never heard it before, either," he said softly, incredulously, and to his immense satisfaction, he heard it again as she clung to him, saying it over and over.

"Stop, angel," he said. "Stop, or I won't be responsible for my actions, and we still have a castle to see today."

Gently, with all the tenderness bursting in his heart, he seated her again, and after shutting her door, got back behind the wheel. He looked at her, at her beautiful face, her eyes wide and loving and trusting on him, and reached out a hand, pulling her close to him. "Let's go back down," he said. "I'll find you another castle, somewhere else, another day, on a road with no edges."

She met his gaze, her eyes steady. "I want to see this castle with you," she said. "Today. I have to go home on Monday."

As if a sledgehammer had slammed into his chest, he realized then what he'd done. He'd fallen in love with a woman who hated his kind of life. He'd fallen in love with a woman who loved him in return. He'd fallen in love with a woman, and even if she had loved his uniform, thought the way he lived perfect, he would still have nothing, nothing at all to offer her, because he would not let anybody he loved be hurt the way he would inevitably hurt her.

He wanted, desperately, to turn back the clock. And he couldn't.

He'd said what he had. She'd said what she had.

And now she sat there, loving him, trusting him, waiting for him to say something about the time beyond Monday. . . .

He squeezed his eyes shut, clenched his fists, wished Monday away, but he knew it was coming, knew he couldn't hold it back. Nor could he hold Sylvia here.

Or anywhere.

"Eric," she said, pressing her soft palm to his cheek, "we have today, love. Let's not waste it worrying."

Opening his eyes, he met her gaze, held it for a long moment, then said, "One castle coming up, angel," and put the car in gear.

As he drove upward, he wished it were a palace and he were a king who could take her there and raise the drawbridge to keep the world at bay, keep her safe in a place where she need never live through any kind of terror again, because she brought to the surface every protective instinct he'd ever had.

And for that reason, he had to send her away.

As they got out of the car at the top of the road, he drew in a deep breath of the fresh, woodsy smell. She was right. They had today. He would not waste it. He slung an arm around her shoulders, and she smiled slowly into his eyes as they walked toward the ticket booth at the base of the wall. "That really wasn't so bad," she said. "You're a very good driver, Eric."

His heart swelled inside his chest until he thought it might burst. He couldn't help himself—he pulled her behind a tree and kissed her soundly for a long, wonderful moment, with her full cooperation and participation.

"Stop," he groaned presently. "If you don't stop, Sylvia, I won't be able to walk and I'll die of starvation, trapped on a hillside under a castle wall."

She laughed and stopped, stepping back from him abruptly. "Why, sir," she said softly, glancing at the front of his pants, "I do believe you *are* in love." Then, with a jaunty swing of her hips that set the hem of her gaudy, calf-length skirt swaying, she walked away, leaving him there for all the world to see.

He caught up to her in three strides, unashamedly hiding behind the folds of her skirt, liking it better every moment. "I thought you couldn't walk," she said. "Maybe your condition isn't terminal after all."

He growled, "Do you want to see this castle, or do you want to discuss my condition?"

"Oh, the castle," she said airily. "I don't think your condition is something we can discuss properly here."

"You've got that right, lady." The look in his eyes told her that when they were in a place where they could "discuss" it, words would play a very small part in their talk.

"Oh, it's so beautiful," Sylvia whispered as she gazed up at the sheer face of ancient gray stone.

He laughed softly. "Why are you whispering?"

Sylvia didn't know, but noticed he spoke in a hushed tone as well. "Maybe because of the ghosts," she said as he took her hand and walked toward a staircase leading up into the dim recesses of the outer wall.

"What ghosts are those?" he asked halfway up, when she paused on a small landing to stand on tiptoe and peer out an arrow slit. The sun slanted in and gilded half her hair, one side of her face, the shoulder of the lemon-yellow blouse she wore with her jungle-print skirt.

She dropped down onto the soles of her sandals as they continued upward. "The ghosts of people who were happy here and come back to visit. And think how many people must have been happy here, how many must have lived and loved and raised families, all blended together, generation after generation, intertwining, overlapping, mingling."

"The women arguing over who was boss of the housekeeping staff, the men fighting duels over who was in charge of the armies, the children bumping one another off in order to inherit," he teased.

"Yucch!" she said, threatening to pitch him down the stairs. "This is my fantasy, mister. If you can't make positive contributions, then keep out of— Oh, my word! Look at the size of this place!"

Sylvia gaped as they came out of the steep staircase onto a terrace where the bulk of the huge structure was far more evident than it had been from below. Two wings angled back from the central tower, each terminating in a tower of its own, and were joined at the rear by another high, crenellated wall. Row upon row of windows slashed deep into the stone walls of the core building, which, like the other towers, was encircled by battlements.

"It must have held hundreds! All those people who tended the farms out there . . ." She gestured to the view of rolling fields, a winding river, and several copses of trees.

"All those people who tended the farms out there lived in abject poverty in mean little hovels," Eric said, and laughed at her outraged expression.

"They were peasants—farmers and hunters—who worked for the landowner and were little more than slaves. They were only permitted inside the castle walls to bring their rents or for protection in times of great danger."

"And for festivals," she argued as they walked slowly toward the rear wall for a better view of the three upper levels. "Celebrations of births and weddings, where they roasted oxen, baked dozens of plump pigeons and haunches of venison. And then there were the fetes to celebrate victories. All the peasants came for those, and dined and danced and made merry, drinking homemade mead."

"In this part of the world, it was more likely bitter black beer, and the peasants would have considered themselves lucky to get the bones from the roasted oxen—the ones the landowner's dogs didn't want—that is, if they'd managed to survive the battles that led to the victory."

She wrinkled her nose. "Battles?"

"There were a lot of battles waged from within these walls. Far more people died here than were ever born."

"I doubt that," she said huffily. "What is it, a male thing to dwell on wars on such a wonderful, sunny day, a quirk of the military mind-set, or is it simply you?"

His lips curled up on one side. Sylvia suppressed the urge to lean forward and kiss him on that corner of his mouth. Lord, how she loved him! Just looking at him made her heart pound too fast. "Merely giving your flights of fancy a touch of historical accuracy," he said.

She stared at him for a moment, exasperation warring with amusement. "But people did *live* here too," she insisted, reminding herself that the differences between a man and a woman were what made relationships exciting—as well as frustrating. "And children were born. It's their souls I sense here, the happy ones, coming back to visit old haunts. Here," she said, striding to a low stone bench beside a deep, dark archway with a heavy wooden and iron door set within, "two maids sit shelling peas into a basin, gossiping about the new stable hand."

Eric stood where she'd left him, the better to watch the breeze press her skirt against her legs and her hair across her cheek.

"The maids were probably sold into service by their starving families," he said, purely to make her eyes flash with annoyance. "Would they be happy enough to want to come back from the afterlife and visit?"

She refused to argue. "Certainly, for their lord and his lady were wonderful, kind masters who made certain the serfs were well fed, properly clothed, and comfortably housed. No hovels for my serfs. Look, those two maids are both wearing shoes and barely patched dresses."

Eric stared and smiled, not at the bench where her gaze rested, but at her, at her childlike enjoyment of this imaginary world she wove.

"And over there"—she indicated a shallow earthen circle in the cobbled floor of the terrace where grass tufted up around an ancient stump—"is an apple tree." Shading her eyes with one hand, she peered more closely into its imaginary limbs. "See? There's a little boy climbing it! Uh-oh, here comes a fat lady in a huge gown and a ruffled wimple. She's the nursemaid, and she's scolding him, telling him to get down."

"Why?" asked Eric, laughing at her. "Isn't he allowed to climb trees?"

"Not in his good clothes," she said, sounding as scandalized as the nursemaid would have, "and he's dressed up in black satin breeches and a white silk shirt because his father, the lord, is due home today from his latest battle."

"Mmm. Phoned ahead, did he?"

Sylvia sniffed. "Don't be silly. A messenger came on the swiftest stallion to tell the baroness, and she's had the staff working since before dawn to prepare a feast for the victorious warriors."

"If he's a lord, why is she a baroness?"

Sylvia giggled. "Because I've never heard of a lordess."

Drawn inexorably by the sunshine in her eyes, Eric stalked toward her, stopped an inch away, and cradled her face in his hands, stroking her hair with both his thumbs where it sprang away from her forehead.

"How do you know the warriors were victorious?"

She backed away from him with a mock-indignant sniff and a toss of her head. "They're coming home, aren't they? Victorious warriors always come home."

If she had chosen her words, Eric thought, feeling an icy hand squeeze his heart even as he squeezed his eyes shut to block out her radiant face, she couldn't have selected any that were more likely to slap him back into reality. What was he doing, letting her play this crazy game, letting her live in this fun-filled fantasy? He should never have told her he loved her, but once he had, he should have made it clear that he couldn't go on doing so, explained to her that it was wrong and he truly did have to find a way to make it stop. Only, he had wanted so badly to pretend that Monday would never come, to forget that their bubble of romantic pretense couldn't last beyond today. Yet pretending was . . . wrong.

"Eric?" Her worried tone forced his eyes open. "What's the matter?"

He realized he was gripping her shoulders too tightly. He relaxed his hold on her, met her gaze, aching deep inside with what he had to do, with what he had to make her see . . . with what he knew he had to destroy!

"Sometimes," he said tautly, "warriors, even victorious ones, don't come home." He was, and she had to be forced to face it, a professional warrior.

He saw understanding of his real meaning dawn, saw her fight it, saw her win the battle and crush it down. She smiled, she tried to laugh, she blinked back the sheen of tears that sprang to her eyes.

"My warriors always win, and they always come home!" she said, struggling not to let the mood escape but knowing it was gone, and that reality had taken its place. Dammit, it had been nothing more than a fantasy! Why did he have to go and ruin it? Why did he have to introduce elements she wasn't prepared to think about?

"Sylvia, I'm talking about reality now," he said, trying to capture her hand. She felt his fingertips slide off her as she spun away from him, marching across the terrace and up the next flight of stairs, where through a narrow window she could see moss and wildflowers and grasses growing in nooks and crannies where stone and mortar had fallen away centuries before—or been shot away by ancient enemy catapults. She glared at him over her shoulder as he followed more slowly, resentful that he'd so forcibly reminded her that wars and death came even to sunshiny terraces and fat ladies and little boys in satin pants.

And to people who believed it could never happen to them. . . .

A sob caught in her throat. She choked it back, but another one pushed it out. As Eric caught up to her, she ran from him, up several stairs, hearing his feet suddenly pounding below her.

"Wait. We have to talk about this," he said, catching the hem of her skirt and holding her back. "Angel, I didn't want to spoil it for you. I didn't mean to make you cry, but . . . we have to face it, Sylvia."

"No, we don't," she said, deliberately misunderstanding. "What do a bunch of ancient warriors matter to us today? Let them go, Eric," she pleaded, turning to look down at him. "Let them rest in peace. Whether they died in battle or in bed, they're all dead anyway, and it doesn't matter anymore." Her voice shook.

"Yes, it does," he said, his own voice none too steady, "because it's not ancient warriors we're talking about, is it? It's me, Sylvia. And how my being what I am would affect you if this . . . this . . . between us . . . went any further."

She said clearly, "This *love* between us, Eric. Why do you find it so difficult to say the word again? And why are you being so negative?"

"It's not a case of being negative. It's a case of facing facts. Because you . . . everyone . . . should maintain a firm grip on reality."

Her eyes flared again as she shook her head, sending tears splashing, shot with gold from a narrow bar of sun that squeezed through a chink in the stone. "There's nothing wrong with my grip on reality." She whipped her skirt from his grip and ran up the last few steps, emerging into the sunlight that danced on her hair, then took up residence in her eyes as she turned to face him again.

"All right, so there were battles here, and people died. But there was happiness too," she said defiantly, blocking his way when he would have come out. "People did live here, did love, did sing and dance and dine. There was revelry as well as strife. Life isn't made up of constant battles. There's good in it as well, but only for those who'll reach out and take it. And that goes for modern times, for you and me, as well as for my lord and his family."

With his hands on her waist, he set her aside so he could step out on the top of the highest tower beside her, with nothing above them but the sky, the white clouds, and the red pennants snapping in the breeze. They were alone.

"I want to reach out," he said, walking her backward as he looked into her eyes. "I tried to. I . . . reached, and found you. Then I realized it was wrong. I . . . can't reach out." She heard the pain in his voice, saw anger boiling in his eyes and didn't know where it was directed . . . except that he was looking at her. "Not to you, of all people," he added.

The sun-warmed rocks of the wall heated her back, but the expression in his eyes chilled her heart. Where had it gone, the immense joy of only moments before? He was in love with her; she was in love with him. And now he was saying, not half an hour after declaring his love, that he couldn't reach out to her. . . .

"Of all people?" she said. "Why *not* me, of all

people? Eric, you said you love me. I'm the one you should reach out to."

"No." He ran a hand over his face. "I should never have told you, Sylvia. I should have simply let you go, because how can I hope to keep you? Oh, God, the letting-go will be much harder now that I've heard you say those words to me."

"Let me go?" Her voice shook. "It sounds more like you mean to *make* me go. Why, Eric?"

"Because I wear a uniform. Because you made it clear from the beginning how you feel about that."

"Eric . . ."

He held up a hand to silence her. "And because I . . . remember my mother screaming."

"That's got nothing to do with us!" she protested.

"Nothing? It has everything to do with us! You, with your perfect childhood, your warm, close-knit family, your life in which the biggest trauma was losing your teddy bear for a few hours, can never understand that kind of loss, or what it does to a woman, to a family!

"Death exists, Sylvia! For a man like me, it hangs out there, waiting, hovering in the background. Did you never consider that if there's a victor, there also has to be a loser? I could have, just as easily as the next guy, been shot down, and I knew it, I accepted it, but . . . only for myself.

"I didn't have to accept it on anybody else's behalf, and I won't. Never."

She was appalled. "Dammit, do you think I'm so shallow, Eric, that I would love only a man who was impervious to death? Do you believe I'm that much of a coward? That's not what I object to in military men! Eric, anybody can die, war or no war, and anyway, that's over."

"Sylvia, Sylvia, you have to face the same facts I'm facing. Sure, that one's over, but how do you know there won't be another one somewhere else next week, or next month, or next year? It's because I . . . care about you that I want you to know what can happen."

"I do know what can happen, Eric. I'm not a fool."

"*She* knew, too, as much as any woman can, yet she married my father and let her life be ruined."

There was such grief in his voice that Sylvia closed her eyes and leaned her head back, shoulders slumping. Slowly, she let her anger trickle away and opened her eyes to see him studying her face, his eyes somber. She ran her fingers up his forearm, to where his shirtsleeve was rolled just above his elbow, then back down again to his fingers, linking hers with him. Did he honestly think her fantasies were anything like his mother's? Was that why he'd become so upset over her castle ghosts? Couldn't he see the difference?

"All right, granted," she said, "your mother lives in a fantasy world—a 'safe and gentle' place, I think you called it—but this is me, Eric." She tapped her chest. "*Me.* I might make up a fantasy now and then, but that doesn't mean I intend to live there forever—or need to."

"I know that. I also know I saw you in the throes of a full-blown anxiety attack," he said. "Over nothing more than an 'edge'! Sylvia, how do you think I'd feel, flying a mission, even a peacetime mission, thinking of you at home, panicky and alone, and me not there for you? What do you think it would do to my concentration? And if something went wrong, would I have to die with the imagined sound of your screams in my ears?"

"No!" she cried, wrenching herself free of him. "I'm not your mother, Eric," she said. "She was asked to face a kind of reality most people never have to confront—and agreed, she did it . . . poorly. But maybe there were things, factors you're unaware of." She knew she should, right now, explain her fear of edges. She knew she should, if she loved him and trusted him as much as she wanted him to love and trust her, tell him the truth. But before she could find the words to begin, he went on.

His square jaw became even stonier than usual. "There were other factors, all right," he said, "and I'm all too aware of them. I grew up on stories of how my mother's breakdown was my father's fault for taking her away from her protective family, dragging her all over the country with him, and then having the gall to die and leave her alone, thousands of miles from home. I don't believe Aunt Freda forgave Charlie for that."

Sylvia could only look at him, feeling helpless. Finally, with a brief touch of her fingers to his face, she said, "It happened so long ago, Eric. Do you have to let it affect you today?"

"It affects me every day."

But never more than today, he thought, this day when he wanted desperately to forget the past and look to the future. But, knowing that the future was a nebulous thing at best, and simply . . . not there at worst, he could only look to what had gone before, what made him the man he was, and try to make Sylvia understand how hopeless it all was.

Sylvia said nothing, only stood watching him, seeing the pain etched in the lines between nose and mouth, the stark shadow of the flagpole bisecting one cheek like a dueling scar. His square chin was unrelentingly stern, his mouth a hard, thin line; his eyes, under lowered brows, seemed to stare into a distance only he could see as he rested his folded arms on the surrounding parapet. Dress him in mail, arm him with a crossbow, and he could have been one of the warriors of her imagination, poised to protect his loved ones from a marauding enemy, determined to win even at the cost of his own life.

"How does it affect you every day?"

He shifted his feet until his back was to the wall. His gaze rested on her face, but she wasn't sure he saw her.

"Ten years ago when I joined the air force," he said slowly, "I was certain I had everything I wanted, was everything I'd ever dreamed of being. There I stood at the threshold of life, freedom at my fingertips, the sky up there waiting, nothing to hold me back. My family no longer needed me, and finally understood what was right for me. For a while, the vagabond life suited me completely. Then it began to pall, and I realized I was lonely. I needed someone to share things with. I started making plans. I had a few years in service, a promotion or two, a pretty good paycheck, and it was time to find a loving lady who wanted to live my kind of life with me.

"We'd have children, I thought." His smile was faint and bitter. "A son named Charlie to start with. I was going to be with him as he grew up, do all the things with him that I wished my father had been able to do with me, from tossing him into the air when he was little to taking him fishing when he was bigger. And then, when the time was right, I was going to teach him to love the sky the way I do, show him what flying can do for the soul, how it makes a man grow, change, see things differently—more clearly, I thought, then."

He turned away to lean on the top of the rampart again, and added softly, almost musingly, "I was going to give him everything," as if he couldn't quite understand where the dreams had gone, or why.

"And what happened?" Sylvia asked when he failed to go on, only stared broodingly out over the fields and forests again. "Did the lady not want your vagabond life?"

Ruefully, he shook his head, glancing sideways at her. "No. There never was a lady. Or if there was, she never crossed my path . . . not at the time when I still believed my own fantasies."

He turned and looked directly, intently, into her eyes, his own so deeply blue she thought she could have dived into them forever and never found bottom. "Do you know what happens when a pilot prangs his plane, even in peacetime?"

Ten

Sylvia looked at him, mystified. "Prangs?"

"Prangs. Thunders in. Goes down." He bit off the words impatiently. "We use euphemisms because we hate the real word. Crashes."

She drew in a sharp breath, remembering those graphic shots on TV of battered pilots. "He . . . ejects."

"He ejects if he can," Eric corrected her firmly. "Sometimes he can't. If he can't, he dies. It's that simple. And when one goes down and a man dies, all too often there is a woman left behind to grieve."

"That's right," she replied. "And an accountant can get hit by a bus on his way to work and there could be a widow left behind to grieve!"

"But in your pleasant little fantasy world, the bus would have better brakes. Sylvia, I'm not blaming you for your inability to understand. I'm simply facing reality—for both of us. You've never faced death, or had to deal with it. Hell, you still have four living grandparents!"

She made a protesting sound. "Eric, you don't know what you're talk—"

"I do know what I'm talking about," he said with gentle insistence. "Listen to me, please. Understand where I'm coming from.

"Several times I've been called upon to go with the padre to a brother officer's house to inform a new widow that her husband's . . . gone.

"They know, those women! Every time! That's what makes the long walk from the car to the front door so terrible, because they always know somehow, when those two uniforms approach, that their lives are about to be shattered. Sometimes they know the minute the staff car pulls up in front of their house. You see an edge of drapery twitch, or a suddenly white face at a kitchen window, and they come to the door with their eyes all big and wounded and their color gone." He gripped her shoulders in both hands and held her before him, eyes burning into hers, looking wounded, and his own color was gone as he stared at her, reliving a particular horror. He pulled in a ragged breath over his teeth, his torture written clearly on his face.

"No one will ever do that to a woman I love, Sylvia. Therefore, I must not love! I meant it when I said I have to find a way to make it stop!"

She wrenched herself free of him. "Then I pity you, Eric Lind! If you won't love, then it's because you're afraid for yourself, not for the poor woman who gets mixed up with you. As I see it, you're too wrapped up in the past even to consider that there might be a decent future waiting for you. That's why you never found your 'loving lady,' because you didn't have the guts to open your eyes and see if she was walking by! Your problem is not that your aunt never forgave your father for dying, but that *you* never did!"

Suddenly, she heard a chatter of voices on the narrow stairs ascending to their level and plunged toward them, ducking under Eric's outstretched arm, flattening herself against the wall as a group of Japanese came streaming upward, led by their guide. When the last of them had passed her position, she continued her headlong flight, and was leaning on the car, much calmer, when Eric appeared.

He ran a hand through his hair and looked at her ruefully.

"I meant it when I said I love you," he said.

She searched his eyes, and nodded. "I know that, Eric." She tried to say more and couldn't, only turned from him and got in the car as he unlocked it.

"By the middle of next month," he said, his hands wrapped tightly around the wheel, "I have to decide whether to sign up again."

"Sign up," she said stonily. "It's your life. It's what you're . . . committed to."

Silently, he put the car in gear and drove to the bottom of the treacherous road, and Sylvia never even flinched. She simply sat there, her face pale, her eyes shaded by her sunglasses.

What have I done? he asked himself. Found love and lost it, all in the same day? Had any man ever been more of a fool?

She couldn't sleep. The room was hot, the air too still. The sheer curtains over the window and the balcony door hung limply. Sylvia sighed and slipped out of bed, went to the door, and leaned on it. Even the glass was warm to the touch. Silently, she opened it and stepped out, walking on bare feet across the blessedly cool tiles of the floor, and leaned on the wall overlooking the front garden. Even without a breeze, the scent of wallflowers wafted upward, thick, rich, intoxicating. Above, a million stars shone down, creating deep, black shadows and casting a silver glow over white roses where moths danced in erratic patterns, fluttering from bush to bush.

A drop of moisture splashed on Sylvia's arm, and she looked at it in surprise, wondering how it could be raining from such a crystal sky. The drop was followed by another, and another, and she didn't bother brushing them away. They had to come. She'd hoped they'd wait until she was home, but if not, there was no point in trying to make them stop. She smiled in spite of them, thinking of Eric's wanting to make love, stop . . . thinking of Eric. He was afraid to go to his death with the sound of her screams in his mind. She was afraid she'd go to hers with him in her mind, period.

Eric lay on his back, his head full of words he would never say, his heart full of pain that would never leave, his mind full of all the things he had said and meant and could never take back, however much he might want to.

Lord, but it was hot! Muggy, too, as if a storm were brewing. Sweat trickled down his spine. He got up, went to the door, and opened it quietly so as not to disturb the sleeping household.

The sleeping woman.

The woman sleeping in the room next door. Who should be sleeping in his bed, in his arms. The woman who he knew without being told was not going to wait until Monday to leave, but would go tomorrow, out of his life. Forever. Because he couldn't think of a way to keep her with him and still be fair to her. Gently, he swept the curtains back. Were hers open? Could he look at her as she lay sleeping, one more time?

He stepped out and came to a halt, seeing her at the edge of the balcony, secure because there was something to hold on to. He ached inside with wanting to spend the rest of his life providing substance for her to cling to when edges loomed large in her mind; he wanted to be the one to comfort her when she feared, bolster her when she faltered. How still she stood, arms folded on the top of the half-wall, her legs in darkness, her nightgown appearing to float there as it hung from her slender shoulders. Then, as if she sensed him there, she turned, and he saw spangles of silver on her pale, perfect face.

His breath caught in his throat. He took a step. Another. Another. And then he swept her into his arms, feeling her tears on his shoulder, her thighs against his, her breasts on his chest, her arms around his waist.

"Make love to me," she said.

"Oh, yes . . ."

His hands traced the shape of her face, his thumbs wiping away her tears, but still they fell, oozing from her eyes as she gazed at him, blinking them away, licking them from her lips, smiling through them for him, her wonderful, special rainbow smile, lit by a million stars. He couldn't bear it. Her smile should have been one of sunshine, pure gold, not one of tears, and he had done this to her, would go on doing it because to do otherwise would surely bring her deeper pain.

He lifted her, carried her back through the open

door to her room, placed her ever so tenderly on the bed, and bent over her. Turning on the pale bedside light, he watched her weep, wanting to weep himself but unable to. His feelings went too deep, were too strong, for that. "I love you," he whispered, lying with her, trailing his hand from her brow to her breast, unbuttoning the front of her thin gown, parting its sides, stroking gentle caresses over her burning skin. He watched her responses, drawing in her scent, seeing her spangled smile soften as she purred her pleasure. Her lips trembled with desire, then parted as she spoke.

"I love you," she said, and he fell onto his back, swinging an arm over his eyes. She knelt at his side, bending close, her hair brushing his skin, sliding her hands over his chest, bending to speak with her lips against one of his nipples. "Eric, my darling, I love you so much. Please, don't let it make you unhappy." Her tears fell on him.

A tearing sound came from his throat, and he wrapped his free hand in her hair, bringing her face to his, holding her tightly as he kissed her until she could hardly draw breath. Breaking free, she continued her exploration of him with gentle hands while he breathed harshly, unevenly, his eyes nearly black with the terrible pain she wanted only to banish.

Deep, sweet emotion that went far beyond the mere physical sensations sweeping over Sylvia welled up and added to the sensuality as she stroked, with hands and lips, his face, his hair, his shoulders, learning again the texture of his skin, the power of his muscles, learning what made him draw in a sharp, harsh breath of ecstasy, what made him sigh, what made him moan. Never had such tenderness toward a man enhanced her love-making. She wanted to give him more pleasure than he'd ever had before, love him better than he'd ever been loved, sear herself onto his soul.

He was naked, erect, wanting her, and she touched him, felt his whole body stiffen. "Do you like that?" she whispered.

"Yes . . ." His breath whistled out on the word. He lay straight and quivering, as if not participating were his punishment for having dared to love, but when she cupped him, testing his weight, his arms snapped down, hands clutching her shoulders, cords in his throat standing out taut as he lifted his head. She smiled again, watching his eyes, and squeezed gently. "And that?"

His breath came in on an agonized gasp. "Angel . . ."

Her tears splashed onto his belly. "What? Do you want me to stop?"

"Don't . . . stop."

"I won't." One hand stroked; the other cradled, squeezed gently again, and he shuddered. "Oh, Lord, you'd better stop!" He grabbed her hands, flipped her onto her back, and leaned over her, pinning her wrists above her head, kissing her damp face, her throat, her shoulders, her breasts. "I love you. I love you. I love you. . . ."

And then, before she was ready, it was moving too fast for her again, raging out of control, and there was no way to slow down even though she wanted to savor every moment of this bliss, make it last for both of them.

His heat, his taste, his scent, filled her, turning her wanton, making her cry out with need for more and more of him, wanting it all now, wanting it forever. She whisked her wrists from his grip and raked her nails lightly down his front, stopping at his navel to explore it gently, then stroked her palm over his hard arousal, pressing hard with the heel of her hand as his hips surged to her caress.

"Sylvia . . ." Eric groaned as she rubbed her cheek, then her lips, across one of his nipples, tongued it and kissed it while she fingered the other one, tugging it between thumb and finger.

This was different, more intense than anything had ever been before, and he lifted his head and smiled at her, seeing that her tears had stopped, knowing she felt the same phenomenal power of this incredibly moving experience they were sharing when she whispered, "I don't want this ever to stop!"

"I know," he said. "I don't either." But he knew it would, knew it had to. His head spun with overwhelming sensations as he read love in her eyes, longing, wanting. "Don't think about its stopping," he whispered against her mouth. "Simply . . . take what there is."

"No," she said. "To you, I want only to give, and give and give." She gave him her breasts, and he took them again with his mouth, until her breath whistled in and out through her throat. She went taut as she flung her head back, for in the giving was greater pleasure than she'd dreamed.

"Sweet," he murmured. "Oh, you taste so sweet."

"You taste salty," she breathed, and he knew salty was good for her because she licked his throat, nibbled on his earlobe, raising goose bumps all over him, making him ache for her touch wherever they rose. He rolled to his side, drawing her long, lean, naked body tightly into his arms, wrapping her with his legs.

"I want you," she said, staring up at him. "Please, Eric, it has to be now."

"Angel . . ." He swallowed hard, forgetting everything but his luck, the blessing of this woman who wanted him as much as he wanted her, a woman he loved, finally, and completely, and irrevocably. And with that love came responsibility, the need to protect, to cherish, to take care of her. He rolled to the bedside table, mentally begging Rob not to let him down in this moment of terrible need; then, moments later, he rose over her, holding back, waiting until he was sure she was ready for him, and plunged deep.

Struggling for a control that slipped further from his grasp with each second, he withdrew, then plunged back into her, feeling her muscles catch him, hold him, reluctantly let him go when he lifted again. She locked him to her as he drove inside her. She was writhing, rocking under him, riding a high crest that he could almost see as her eyes went wide, then squeezed tightly shut as, on a low, glad cry, her face went slack and her body rigid, trembling so hard in his arms he thought she might break.

"I love you!" The words were wrenched from him as her climax sent him over the edge and he followed her, gasping for breath; then slowly, gently, he coasted back down to rest on her for several moments before rolling to the side, carrying her with him. She smiled at him, touched his face, whispered his name, and closed her eyes, and he noticed, on a level that was not quite consciousness, that her tears had begun again.

A long time later Sylvia opened her eyes and smiled at Eric, saw the same emotions in his eyes that washed her every pore, watched him try to speak, fail, shake his head, and close his mouth, and knew there were no words in any language to explain the depths of their feelings.

Closing her eyes, she ran a hand slowly over his shoulder, delighting in the sensation of his skin, smooth and sleek under her palm, then continued down his arm, feeling the thickening hair as she neared his wrist where it rested on her hip. His biceps were powerful, his forearm sinewy, the back of his hand filled with knobby knuckles, over which she stroked a gentle finger. He drew in a deep breath and let it out on a long, trembling sigh, and she opened her eyes to look at him, seeing the love in his eyes, and the sorrow.

Wordlessly, she watched him as he lay on his side, elbow bent, head propped on one fist, looking at her so sadly that she ached all over. He kissed her brow, her cheek, her lips, softly, whispering his words of love. Then, silently, with deliberate slowness, making it last as long as they could, they loved each other again with a deep intensity that left both of them shaken.

When it was over, he left her there, and she buried her face in the pillow, drawing in deep lungfuls of his scent. Was this all there was going to be? All she would have of him?

Would this have to last a lifetime?

She wanted to argue, to rail against fate and use physical violence to fight for what was hers, but what was the point in trying to oppose someone with a rigid mind, a man who could see only one path? What good would it do?

Eleven

Sylvia slumped against the door frame and stood silently, watching her mother tapping away at her portable typewriter perched on the edge of the picnic table in the backyard. "Hi, Mom." Her mother turned, startled, and jumped to her feet, meeting Sylvia at the bottom of the steps leading down from the porch.

"Sylvia! Oh, I'm so glad you're home! How was your trip? Come inside out of this heat. I just made a fresh jug of lemonade. Have you eaten? Do you want some lunch? Or maybe just a snack to hold you till dinnertime?"

"No." Sylvia's voice was a sad little croak. "Oh, Mom . . . I need a hug."

With tea and tears, in fits and starts, with long pauses and great spates of angry, anguished words, the story emerged. Her mother listened in a sympathetic, encouraging silence. Then, after a thoughtful pause, she said, "Tell me this one thing, Sylvia. Does he hang up his pants . . . first?"

Sylvia stared at her mother in amazement and felt a hot blush rising in her face.

"Mo-om . . ."

"Now, darling, you're thirty years old, not fifteen. Answer my question. You don't have to tell me the answer, only yourself. And if it's what I think it is, your Eric is no more totally rigid than your father is. He probably has his impetuous side, his own little spontaneities."

Sylvia stared. "Impetuous? Old Meat-Loaf-Because-It's-Friday? Mr. Why-Eat-Dinner-in-the-Backyard-When-We-Have-a-Perfectly-Good-Dining-Room? Spontaneous? Dad?"

Her mother only smiled, and a certain quality in that smile made Sylvia stare at her in delighted disbelief. Her father *still* didn't hang up his pants first?

"Even after thirty-five years?" she asked.

Her mother nodded, looked down, and a hint of color stained her cheeks. "There are . . . other things, too, dear. But that's always been one of my favorites."

"Oh, Mom. Why did I never ask you before why your marriage to a man so different from you worked so well? And why didn't I recognize that the things I love about Eric are probably the same things you love about Dad?"

"Did you have fun with Eric? Did you laugh together? Does he have a sense of humor? Your dad and I always have so much fun together. He's my best friend."

Sylvia said slowly, understanding dawning. "Yes . . . yes, he's lots of fun to be with." She dried her eyes, blew her red nose, leaned back her head, and laughed. "Oh, yes, we had fun. Our first lunch together was a picnic in the woods. Even if he had a linen tablecloth, real knives, and crystal wineglasses, the mustard, at least, came right out of a jar." Her eyes softened, misted over again. "And he laughed like a lunatic when the puppy peed on his foot."

"See?" said her mother, and Sylvia nodded.

Could a man who didn't hang up his pants . . . first, ever be considered truly rigid in mind-set?

Of course not. Hidden somewhere inside Eric Lind's very proper uniform was a man who wore red shirts on his day off, a man whose sneakers should have been buried years ago, a man who got carried away necking in a car in broad daylight, a man who ate giant cream puffs messily in public, a man who liked poems that rhymed. A man her mother would love.

A man who fell in love at first sight, even if he admitted it only with reluctance. A man worth fighting for, even if he was the one she had to fight.

But for all that, Sylvia thought as she drove back to her apartment that evening, with Froggie in a pet box in the backseat, she still didn't know what to do about fixing the rift between herself and Eric, because there were problems other than his wearing a uniform, difficulties that went beyond any imagined rigidity on his part. Even if she fought him and won, made him change his mind and decide he could live with the threat of his own mortality and what it might mean to her, could she fight the fear in her own heart, the fear that she had to admit now had sent her flying home instead of staying to battle it out with him?

She would have won. She, and his love for her, would have made it impossible for him to resist, if she had forced the issue. But she hadn't.

Why?

Because, when all was said and done, she was a coward.

"I'm sorry, sir. I can't give out Ms. Mathieson's home address or phone number. It's against company policy."

Eric leaned toward the woman behind the name-plate on the reception desk. "Ms. Chang, it is of vital importance that I know." He slowly drew himself up to his full height and squared his shoulders inside his uniform jacket. "It's a matter of national security."

"Really." Ms. Chang was not impressed. She chewed a pencil. Eric was sure it was to hide a smile. "And what would Sylvia Mathieson have to do with national security?"

Oh. He hadn't expected that kind of question. "Uh . . . security forbids my telling you."

"Uh-huh." She dropped the pencil and smiled. "If you were really with national security, you'd have other methods of finding her. There are reasons for our policy, Captain Lind, and men like you are among them. You can wait here if you want. She may be in before closing time. If not, then you can come back tomorrow and wait again, but I am not telling you where she lives."

With that, Ms. Chang turned back to her type-writer and began hitting the keys, creating a small storm of sound that Eric listened to stoically for the next three and a half hours. When it stopped and Ms. Chang stood, put a cover on the type-writer, and carried a stack of papers into an inner office, he got to his feet, eyeing the big filing cabinet that her desk guarded.

What information might it hold? He stepped

back guiltily, not realizing how close to those files he'd moved until Ms. Chang came out of another room, her purse slung over her shoulder, a big ring of keys in her hand. "Shall we go?" she asked, bouncing the keys teasingly.

She held open the door for him. He was stiff and sore from spending half a day on a plastic chair. He watched her carefully lock the door, then followed her down the stairs to the lobby. She let him out, shut the door carefully behind her, and locked it, too, before offering Eric a lift . . . somewhere. With equal politeness, he declined, tipped his uniform cap in farewell, and strode away, arms swinging at exactly the correct degree of incline, an officer on parade, a fine, upstanding citizen . . . with larceny on his mind.

Getting through the outer door was the most difficult, but only because the street was busy and opportunities to work unobserved were few until about 3:00 A.M. He picked the lock quickly at that point, easing into the lobby, waiting for a clanging alarm. None sounded. The stairwell had an echoing, empty building sound to it as he ran up the one flight and crouched outside her office door. That lock was a touch harder, but it gave. The real toughie, oddly enough, was the filing cabinet because it was so simple it was tempting to break it instead of gently slipping its single tumbler out of the way with a twist of his probe; but then it was done.

Personal . . . Personnel . . . Payroll. Where to look? Nowhere in that cabinet was there anything with so much as Sylvia's name on it. Flipping through, thinking fast, he found the file without knowing it at first.

Taxes: Business, personal.

He had only just started reading with the help of his little flashlight when the door behind him burst open and two armed men leapt into the room, shouting "Freeze!" They fanned out, one below the level of the desk, the other exposed for only a moment as he sought the protection of a huge tub in which a leafy tree grew. As Eric froze, a third armed man pointed a gun at him from the doorway.

He let the tax file slither to the floor, staring into a barrel that looked about as big around as a garden hose, saying—and feeling utterly foolish as he did so—"Honestly, Officer. I can explain. . . ."

Sylvia couldn't stop shaking as she stared at Eric where he sat on a stool in the downtown police station, to which she had been called to "identify an intruder caught in her office, who claimed to know her." His hands were still cuffed behind him.

"I'm sorry, Officer," she said. "It's all my fault. I forgot to tell Captain Lind where the alarm is so he could, uh, shut it off. You see, I only had it installed a month ago, and I sometimes forget myself that it's there and only remember when I get into my own office and see the little red light flashing at me to remind me and . . ." Sylvia sighed, knowing she was talking too much, knowing that giving no explanation at all would be better than offering this lame and convoluted one, knowing that no one believed her anyway, but she couldn't seem to stop babbling. "When I gave him my office keys, I should have—"

"Sylvia. They've already relieved me of my lock picks."

She stared at him. *Lock picks?* "Someday," she said, "you're going to have to tell me more about those summer jobs of yours." His eyes asked her if there were really going to be a "someday" for them. Her mouth trembled, not knowing whether to laugh or weep, say yes or no. "Let him go, please," she begged the officer who seemed to be in charge. "He was only trying to find me because . . ." She looked at Eric. "Because . . . ?"

He gazed at her, as if he didn't know exactly why himself, and when she looked back at the policeman and again said, "Please," he released Eric into her custody.

"I think I must own you now," she said something short of an hour later as she looked at the sheaf of papers she'd dumped on the coffee table in her apartment. "I never knew there'd be so much trouble involved in springing the guy who tripped my alarm."

He searched her face. "*Too* much trouble?"

She shook her head and lowered herself carefully to the couch behind her, as if she were afraid something might break if she moved too fast. Her eyes never left his face for an instant. "No. If you could go to all the trouble of picking my locks, then I guess I can take the time to listen to an explanation of why."

He stood there, almost at attention, looking very military in spite of the second-story-man black pants, black turtleneck, and broken-down tennis shoes that let his toes stick out. "Because I had to find your address. I needed to see you. I couldn't wait. I love you."

She nodded. "I believe we've already established that."

"You're not going to make this easy for me, are you?"

"It . . . isn't easy, Eric. The easy thing would be to drag you into my bedroom and . . . you know."

"Yeah. I know." His tone was dry, his eyes somber, as he sat on the far end of the sofa from her, leaning his elbows on his knees, his hands hanging down between. "I signed up for another term before I left Germany. I'll be posted sometime within the next month or two. I don't know where I'll be going."

"Military men seldom do."

"But military families . . . survive." There was a certain element of doubt in his tone.

"Some of them," she acknowledged cautiously.

"If a man had a strong wife, his family would have a better chance, wouldn't it?"

"Probably." She met his gaze. "The husband would need to be strong, too, Eric. He'd need to trust his wife."

"Have faith in her, you mean? Faith that she wouldn't let him down." He hesitated. "Or his—their—children if it . . . it came to . . . to the crunch."

She fixed him with her gaze. "No euphemisms, Eric."

He drew in an unsteady breath. "If he gets killed."

"Yes. A man would need that kind of faith as much as a woman would need all of her strength."

He searched her face. She felt everything in him reaching out to everything in her, but she still had to hold back, too filled with her own uncertainties to take what he offered. Even when he said, "I have that kind of faith in you, that depth of trust," she wondered if her faith, her trust, was enough. And her strength.

"That's why I came," he said. "I had to tell you. To . . . ask you."

"Ask me what?"

His eyes were dark blue, deeply intense. "To marry me. To help me make sense of it all. To spend the rest of your life with me. I'm not really a rigid man. I'd try to make life . . . fun for you and our children, not live by the numbers."

"I know," she said. "I already had that figured out. I think I knew before I left that you aren't a rigid person."

He frowned. "You did? Then . . . why did you let me send you away, Sylvia?"

She got to her feet. Confession time.

"I didn't let you 'send' me away, Eric. I left. Because I was afraid to stay and fight."

He rose too. Did she know, he wondered, how short a battle it would have been? How easily she would have won? "Why? Because I wear a uniform?"

She shook her head and backed away from him. "No. That was only an excuse." She searched his eyes for a long moment. "Because I'm not . . . strong, and I know you have a certain contempt for cowards. I probably knew it then, but I hadn't sorted it out in my own mind, so I let myself believe that I was leaving because you didn't want me."

"Never that," he said, striding toward her, but she held him back with an upraised hand.

"No. Please. I have something to tell you, Eric, something I'm terribly ashamed of, something that hurts me very much, but you have a right to know, because until you know that about me, you don't know me. You can't make a proper judgment about wanting me for your wife."

She swallowed several times, opened her mouth to speak, and closed it again.

Eric took one of her icy hands between his, watching her, waiting. "Nothing is going to make me love you less."

"I told you I was in love before," she said. "That I wanted to marry the man, have his babies." She sent a small, twisted smile his way.

"Shane?" he asked, his voice suddenly harsh.

She blinked in astonishment. "No!"

"All right. Go on."

"His name was Dean Edderly. But it turned out he didn't need my babies because . . ." Her mouth trembled. He saw shame flood her eyes, along with agony. "Because he already had one of his own . . . and another one on the way."

"Sylvia . . . angel, you had no way of knowing that." He didn't know where the conviction came from that she'd been innocent in the matter, but it was there, and he went with it.

"That's what I tell myself, but there must have been clues I was simply too unperceptive to see. I went up to Whistler with him one afternoon. We were going to spend a couple of days in a house he was marketing—he was in real estate—and I had every hope that during that time he'd ask me to marry him." She pulled her hand from Eric's clasp. "I was so . . . confident!"

"But?" he encouraged her quietly.

"But somebody . . . somebody brought him a message . . . from his wife, a message telling him she was pregnant. She'd phoned his office to tell him because she was so happy, and they gave her my number as one of the places he'd said he could be reached. He phoned there, and Shane answered the phone. . . ." Her voice shook. "Shane, my brother, my twin, the other side of my soul."

She backed away from Eric when he would have held her. "He came after us, Shane did. After me, to tell me what kind of man I was involved with, and after Dean, to give him the message." She laughed, a small, sad, croaking sound. "He gave it to him all right, right between the eyes, and hauled me out of that house into his car."

Her face paled. Her respiration grew shallow. Sweat beaded her forehead. Eric reached for her, but she paced to the other side of the room, her hands twisting. "He shouldn't have been driving. He was too upset. Oh, heavens, but he was mad! He was driving too fast—he always did. We both did, but that time the road was icy. I begged him to slow down. It's steep up there. Twisty. The car slid on a corner and we went . . . over the . . . over the . . ."

"Over the edge," Eric said quietly, mostly to himself, as understanding came, leaving him feeling sick and inadequate and helpless.

She nodded, her gaze clinging to his face. "And into a deep gully. I can still feel it, still see it." Her tone was flat as she pressed herself against a wall, her hands spread, fingers curled, as if she were clinging to it for protection. "We . . . the car . . . turned over twice in the air, and it happened so slow I saw Shane's face in the glow of the headlights as they bounced off the snow, once, and once again. He looked so surprised. Not frightened like I was, not screaming. Just . . . surprised, as if he were going on a huge adventure . . . and then there was . . . noise, crashing, trees breaking, metal tearing—and then it was quiet. Shane still had that same wondrous look on his face. He was dead."

Eric groaned and covered his eyes with one hand. "I said you didn't know death."

"I know death. Intimately." Her expressionless, even tone brought his burning eyes back to her. "I lay there upside down with it for two and a half days." She met his eyes from across the room. "I . . . screamed a lot. That's why I talk funny even now. I damaged my vocal cords, screaming. Like your mother screamed."

"For help," he croaked.

"Yes. Of course." Her clawed hands relaxed their attempt to cling to a flat wall. "That's probably why she screamed, too, Eric. For help."

He nodded as he stood there shaking. His knees were weak. He looked at her, saw her need, her vulnerability . . . and her strength, and felt power come back to his legs. "I guess I didn't understand that. Until now."

He paced toward her, his steps slow, sure, and stopped half an arm's length away when her eyes told him to. "I understand a lot more now."

"But . . . not all of it, not yet. Dean followed us that night, Eric. He followed right behind Shane's car."

Eric stared. "What are you saying? You screamed for help for two days down in the bottom of a gorge and the man had watched you go over? He didn't report it?"

"That's right. You see, he had a commitment to his wife and children. He came to see me in the hospital later and tried to explain. He hadn't realized how much they meant to him until he thought he might lose them. If he'd reported the accident, she'd have known he wasn't where he'd said he was going to be."

"No!" Eric railed against the notion. "It's unconscionable! He could have reported it anonymously! He could have . . ." He sighed. "He didn't. All right. I guess I have to accept that. He simply . . . didn't?"

"That's right. He didn't. He made a choice, you see. Between me and her. When the chips were down, he went with the commitment that was closest to his heart, the one that meant the most to him. And he was right. Oh, not right to leave us there, Shane and me, but right to stay with his wife." She lifted her chin, challengingly, Eric thought, and added softly, pointedly, "After all, he was married to her."

Understanding dawned in him, leaving him feeling sick and sad and inadequate again. "And I told you I was married, didn't I? Married to the air force."

She nodded. "That's why I left Germany without fighting for you, Eric. Not because of your uniform, not because you're so very rigid, because you're not. I left because I'm a coward. I was afraid of your strong commitment to something other than me. I was . . . jealous."

"And now?"

Her voice trembled slightly, but she spoke over that. "I'm still jealous. Still afraid. But if you want me, knowing what you know, then I'm yours. I'll try to grow stronger, try not to worry that you'll always love your first 'wife' more than you love me. Because doing without your love is worse than anything else I can imagine."

Her eyes gave him the permission he'd been waiting for, and he drew her close. "My love is something you won't have to do without as long as

I draw breath, angel. My strongest commitment will always be to you."

"No. You don't have to say that. Remember, I know what it's like, the military life. Orders are orders. All that comes first."

"Not with me. If you want me to, I'll break my contract with the air force. Today or next year or whenever. I'll live where you want—next door to your folks if that's what you need to make you happy, or on the moon, or in a refrigerator box in the park. Wherever, Sylvia, as long as you're there."

With a sigh she melted against him. "I love you," she said, and kissed him.

A long time later, he lifted his head and smiled at her. "Now do we get to the easy part?"

Her gaze swung to her bedroom door, showing him where it was. "Now we get to the easy part." As she spoke, he lifted her off her feet. Just then the sun came up, slanting in through a crack in the drapes, dancing into her eyes with a pure golden light that took its place in Eric's heart, filling it to the brim.

THE EDITOR'S CORNER

Next month LOVESWEPT celebrates heroes, those irresistible men who sweep us off our feet, who tantalize us with whispered endearments, and who challenge us with their teasing humor and hidden vulnerability. Whether they're sexy roughnecks or dashing sophisticates, dark and dangerous or blond and brash, these men are heartthrobs, the kind no woman can get enough of. And you can feast your eyes on six of them as they alone grace each of our truly special covers next month. HEARTTHROBS—heroes who'll leave you spellbound as only real men can.

Who better to lead our HEARTTHROBS lineup than Fayrene Preston and her hero, Max Hayden, in **A MAGNIFICENT AFFAIR**, LOVESWEPT #528? Max is the best kind of kisser: a man who takes his time and takes a woman's breath away. And when Ashley Whitfield crashes her car into his seaside inn, he senses she's one sweet temptation he could go on kissing forever. But Ashley has made a habit of drifting through her life, and it'll take all of Max's best moves to keep her in his arms for good. A magnificent love story, by one of the best in the genre.

The utterly delightful **CALL ME SIN**, LOVESWEPT #529, by award-winner Jan Hudson, will have you going wild over Ross Berringer, a Texas Ranger as long and as tall as his twin brother, Holt, who thrilled readers in **BIG AND BRIGHT**, LOVESWEPT #464. The fun in **CALL ME SIN** begins when handsome hunk Ross moves in next door to Susan Sinclair. He's the excitement the prim bookstore owner has been missing in her life—and the perfect partner to help her track down a con artist. But once Ross's downright neighborly attention turns Susan inside out with ecstasy, she starts running scared. How Ross unravels her intriguing mix of passion and fear is a sinfully delicious story you'll want to read.

Doris Parmett outdoes herself in creating a perfect HEARTTHROB in **MR. PERFECT**, LOVESWEPT #530. Chase Rayburn is the epitome of sex appeal, a confirmed bachelor who can charm a lady's socks off—and then all the rest of her clothes. So why does he feel wildly jealous over Sloan McKay's personal ad on a billboard? He's always been close to his law partner's widow and young son, but he's never before wanted to kiss Sloan until she melted with wanton pleasure. Shocking desire, daring seduction, and a friendship that deepens into love—a breathtaking combination in one terrific book.

Dangerously sexy, his gaze full of delicious promises, Hunter Kincaid will have you dreaming of **LOVE AND A BLUE-EYED COWBOY**, LOVESWEPT #531, by Sandra Chastain. Hunter knows he can win the top prize in a motorcycle scavenger hunt, but he doesn't count on being partnered with petite, smart-mouthed Fortune Dagosta. A past sorrow has hardened Hunter's heart, and the last person he wants for a companion for a week is a beautiful woman whose compassion is easily aroused and whose body is made for loving. Humorous and poignant, the sensual adventure that follows is a real winner!

Imagine a man who has muscles like boulders and a smoky drawl that conjures up images of rumpled sheets and long, deep kisses—that's Storm Dalton, Tami Hoag's hero in **TAKEN BY STORM**, LOVESWEPT #532. A man like that gets what he wants, and what he wants is Julia McCarver. But he's broken her heart more than once, and she has no intention of giving him another chance. Years of being a winning quarterback has taught Storm ways to claim victory, and the way he courts Julia is a thrilling and funny romance that'll keep you turning the pages.

Please give a rousing welcome to new author Linda Warren and her first LOVESWEPT, **BRANDED**, #532, a vibrantly emotional romance that has for a hero one of the most virile rodeo cowboys ever. Tanner Danielson has one rule in life: Never touch another man's wife. And though he wanted Julie Fielding from the first time he saw her, he never tasted her fire because she belonged to another. But now she's free and he isn't waiting a moment longer. A breathlessly exciting love story with all the wonderfully evocative writing that Linda displayed in her previous romances.

On sale this month from FANFARE are three marvelous novels. **LIGHTS ALONG THE SHORE,** by immensely talented first-time author Diane Austell, is set in nineteenth-century California, and as the dramatic events of that fascinating period unfold, beautiful, impetuous Marin Gentry must face up to the challenges in her turbulent life, including tangling with notorious Vail Severance. Highly acclaimed Patricia Potter delivers **LAWLESS,** a poignant historical romance about a schoolteacher who longs for passionate love and finds her dreams answered by a coldhearted gunfighter who's been hired to drive her off her land. In **HIGHLAND REBEL,** beloved author Stephanie Bartlett whisks you away to the rolling hills and misty valleys of the Isle of Skye, where proud highland beauty Catriona Galbraith is fighting for her land and her people, and where bold Texas rancher Ian MacLeod has sworn to win her love.

Also available this month in the hardcover edition from Doubleday (and in paperback from FANFARE in March) is **LUCKY'S LADY** by ever-popular LOVESWEPT author Tami Hoag. Those of you who were enthralled with the Cajun rogue Remy Doucet in **THE RESTLESS HEART,** LOVESWEPT #458, will find yourself saying Ooh la la when you meet his brother, Lucky, for he is one rough and rugged man of the bayou. And when he takes the elegent Serena Sheridan through a Louisiana swamp to find her grandfather, they generate what *Romantic Times* has described as "enough steam heat to fog up any reader's glasses."

Happy reading!

With warmest wishes,

Nita Taublib

Nita Taublib
Associate Publisher/LOVESWEPT
Publishing Associate/FANFARE

Don't miss these fabulous Bantam Fanfare titles
on sale in JANUARY.

LIGHTS ALONG THE SHORE
by Diane Austell

LAWLESS
by Pat Potter

HIGHLAND REBEL
by Stephanie Bartlett

Ask for them by name.

LIGHTS ALONG THE SHORE

BY DIANE AUSTELL

The Gentrys. They had left the comforts of the Old South and come to California, a sunlit Eden where ranchers put down roots and grew wealthy, while beautiful young women such as Marin Gentry danced until dawn and dreamed of undying love. But ahead was turmoil no man or woman could foresee: the discovery of gold, with its lure of easy money and easier death, the dizzying growth of bawdy San Francisco, the gathering stormclouds of Civil War. . . .

*   *   *

Marin Severance is reunited with her brother-in-law, Vail, for the first time since the night, several years before, when she was still unmarried, and he seduced her. . . .

Stuart had gone to San Francisco four days ago to buy parts for the water pump, and she expected him home for supper.

There were sounds of horses pounding past the side of the house and Stuart's voice calling to Mateo. Then boots on the wooden floor of the back porch and the kitchen door banging open. Marin swung around with flour still on her hands and a smile of greeting on her face. Coming in the door were Stuart, Michael, and, just behind them, Vail Severance.

She picked up a towel, wiped her hands, and moved to Stuart for a kiss of welcome. She said something to Michael, although she couldn't hear her own voice for the roaring in her ears.

What could she do? Where could she look? She must speak to him, look at him, smile at him. It would seem very odd if she didn't. But all the blood in her body seemed to have rushed into her head. Oh, God, how could she explain to Stuart why the sight of his brother upset her so? She forced herself to look into Vail's eyes, and the buzzing in her head made her think she was going to faint.

There was nothing at all in those clear gray eyes but friendliness and the mildest sort of interest, the kind of interest a man might show on greeting his brother's wife, a girl he had known slightly at some time in the distant past. She put out her hand because she had to, felt the corners of her mouth go up in a smile, and heard him say, "Hello, Red."

Somewhere she found the strength to say, "Welcome, Vail. Have you come home to stay?"

Supper went off smoothly, and by the time Luz served the cobbler and cream, Marin had decided that she was going to live after all. Stuart appeared to have noticed nothing odd about her behavior, perhaps because he had been pulling off his coat when she spoke to Vail and had his back turned. Michael had simply stood there and smiled as he always did when he saw her, and as for Vail—Papa and Ethan had clearly been right about the memory-destroying properties of alcohol, for he obviously recalled nothing about that night. He treated her just as he always had, perhaps a little more courteously because of her increased age and status, but that was all. . . .

After supper Marin sat down by the parlor fire in her favorite chair, the one Rose had used in the old days, and picked up a shirt of Stuart's to mend, thinking with relief that she now had a little time to compose herself. She looked up, and the thread snapped in her fingers. Vail had come into the room alone.

Damn the man! Why couldn't he go look at the horse or the pump, or tend to some other masculine matter? Why did he have to follow her in here, where there was no one else to share the burden of conversation? The business of rethreading the needle took her close attention, but she watched him covertly, noticing the way he moved, the vitality in his face.

He sat down opposite her and stretched his booted legs toward the flames, and she busied herself with the torn frill of Stuart's shirt, wondering how long she could maintain this domestic pose and make some kind of polite conversation.

Her mind fumbled, searching for something to say, and Petra came in with her gliding, boneless walk. She set the tray bearing coffeepot and cups on the table next to Marin and, as she bent forward, murmured, "Carey is still awake, Miss Marin. Should I bring him down?"

Marin snatched at the suggestion like a drowning man at a straw. Young as he was, Carey, had a gift for drawing all eyes to him—in this case, away from her.

"Yes, bring him down," she said gratefully.

"How is my mother?" Vail asked suddenly. He was lighting a cigar and frowning into the fire.

It was a safe subject. "Not well," Marin answered, her eyes on her sewing. "Will you see her before you leave?"

"I can't."

She looked up, thinking of Ethan. It was such a sorry, stupid situation. "Surely your father wouldn't object? She's quite ill, I think."

"He would object—which would make it worse for her." A smile crossed his face, and Marin caught her breath at the bitterness in it. Without watching her hand, she shoved the needle through the cloth and jabbed her finger. A bright drop of blood appeared, and she scowled and put it to her mouth.

Vail's smile became genuine. "You looked like a child when you did that. I keep forgetting how young you are."

It was the first personal remark he'd made, and it unnerved her so much that she almost dropped the shirt. He must not have noticed though, for he went right on, "This is the first chance I've had to apologize for my conduct the night of Celia's party. I was very rude."

The finger remained in her mouth; her heart seemed to come to a standstill. He did remember, then, and he was apologizing for *rudeness*?

She was not thinking clearly, but she heard him say, "I had a bad case of hurt feelings that night, as you probably know, and I'm sorry to say I got very drunk. I seem to remember leaving you on the dance floor with Gerald Crown, which I certainly would never have done in my right mind. I hope you've forgiven me."

Her heart began to beat again. He thought he'd left her with Gerald.

"Oh, I forgave you immediately. Gerald is charming and a very good dancer." She picked up the coffeepot and began to pour with a steady hand.

He winced. "I deserved that. My brother married a quick-witted lady as well as a beautiful one. I wasn't so lucky."

He was thinking of Celia. Should she mention her? No, better not. Petra brought in Carey, and Marin took him on her lap with relief. Vail leaned forward and looked him over.

"A handsome boy," he said finally.

She warmed to the praise, as she always did to any kind words for Carey.

"Yes," she said, and laughed. "Forgive me, I can't be modest. I think he's handsome, too." She set the child on the floor, and he immediately went up on all fours and started to rock so vigorously that he tumbled over and lay there crowing. Then he struggled up and tried again to move forward.

Vail took his cup, watching with a smile.

"I suppose Father is delighted."

"Oh, yes. He was miffed at first when we didn't name the

baby after him, but he got over it when he decided that Carey looked like him. At present he's very pleased with me."

"And with Stuart, too, I imagine. Well, Stuart always had the knack of pleasing him. I never did." He said it without self-pity, but Marin remembered Celia's words: "His father hurt him badly."

She picked up her own cup. "Except for your mother, no one agrees with him. My mother thinks Carey strongly resembles her family, the Landrinis, and my father says he looks like me."

Carey raised his head as if he knew he was being discussed, and Vail watched him, moved—even more than he had expected—by emotions hard to analyze. Shame at what he had done to this girl, so innocent and so drunk—it had all been his fault. Respect for her cool courage when she first saw him in the kitchen and her poker player's skill when she showed him her baby. Surprising sadness at the knowledge that, for the baby's sake and for hers, he could never claim the boy as his own. Wonder at the simple fact of the child. There might be other children in the world who were his, but none he knew of, none so certain as this little boy looking up at him with great black eyes shining.

He said, "Your father is right. At least he has his mother's wonderful eyes."

Carey spared her the necessity of a reply. He made a tremendous effort, lifted one tiny hand, brought it forward, and moved the knee behind it. Then he moved the other hand and knee, lifted his head, and chortled.

"Oh!" Marin breathed. "He's done it, he's crawling. Oh, he's been trying so hard!"

Carey began to move faster and faster now that he had figured out the difficult business, traveling in a circle with a triumphant gurgling laugh until he fell in a heap at Vail's feet. Immediately he got up and sat down again with a plop. The man above him extended a finger for him to tug, and the child examined it interestedly, talking to himself in a cooing babble.

Vail looked down at the soft, dark curls. "So now I am an uncle. God, it makes me feel old."

"Ethan is an uncle, too, but he doesn't know it."

"No word at all?"

"Nothing. I think about the knife fights and the hangings in the gold camps. Sometimes I'm afraid . . ."

"Don't be. Ethan can take care of himself. He's a good man in a fight, but he doesn't look for trouble."

"It need never have happened. Papa will never be well, and Mama—she is not herself at all. It was all so stupid . . ."

"Tragedies usually are, because people are stupid. I'm in the camps fairly often. I have business there at times. Ever since I heard about Ethan, I've kept an eye out for him, and I'll continue to."

With a rush of gratitude she said, "Oh, it would mean so much just to know that he's alive, even if he doesn't come home." Impulsively she added, "It's a shame Logan didn't know you were coming. Next time let us know, and I'll make sure she's here."

Why had she said that? Only minutes before she had been hoping never to see this man again, and now she had invited him to come back and to meet Logan in her home, which would make an enemy of Malcolm if he found out. No help for it now. She couldn't take back the invitation, not with him smiling at her like that and the warm light again in his eyes.

"That's very kind. I worry about Logan, trapped in that house."

"There's no place else she'd want to be, not now, with her mother sick. But—do come back. Seeing you will help her, I'm sure of that."

LAWLESS

BY PATRICIA POTTER

Author of RAINBOW

"One of the romance genre's finest talents . . ."
—Romantic Times

IN LAWLESS, Patricia Potter tells the dramatic and compelling story of a brave schoolteacher and the lawless outcast who becomes her protector. When Willow Taylor refuses to sell her land to powerful rancher Alex Newton, legendary gun-fighter Lobo is hired to drive her away. But his attempts go awry as he ends up rescuing members of her "family" from disasters, including a fire. Worse, he's shocked to discover that Willow is unlike the heartless women he's known only too well. As more gunslingers arrive, wreaking havoc in a once peaceful community, Willow remains undaunted, and Lobo feels the heat of unbidden longing for this strong and beautiful survivor.

In the following excerpt, Lobo has broken off with Newton and has temporarily sided with Willow. Under a velvet-dark sky, he finds himself opening up to her as he never had with anyone before. . . .

*   *   *

"Why do they call you Lobo?"

He shrugged. "The Apache gave me the name. It seemed as good as any."

"As good as Jess," she asked, using his real name.

He scowled. "I told you he died."

Willow didn't say anything, but the silence was heavy with her doubt.

He turned away from her. "Lobo fits, lady. Believe me."

"The wolf is a social animal," Willow said as if reading out of a book. "He mates for life."

Lobo turned and stared at her icily. "Unless he's an outcast, chased from the pack, and then he turns on his own kind." There was no self-pity in the observation, only the cold recital of fact.

"Is that what happened?"

Lobo felt his gut wrench. He'd never meant to say what he had, had not even consciously thought it before. A cold dread seeped through him as he realized how much control of himself he was losing.

"Lady, I've done things that would make you puke. So why don't you go back to your nice little house and leave me alone."

Willow hesitated. She sensed the turmoil in him, and it echoed her own churning emotions.

"I don't care about the past," she finally said.

He laughed roughly. "I don't scare you at all?"

She knew he wanted her to say yes. She knew she should say yes. She should be fearful of someone with his reputation, his life. But she wasn't.

"No," she answered.

"You don't know me, lady."

"Willow."

He shook his head. "And the last thing you should do is be out here with me."

"Were you with the Apache long?" she asked softly.

It was a sneaky question, and he stiffened. "Long enough."

She sensed his withdrawal, if it was possible that he could distance himself any farther than he already had. The kiss might never have happened, except it was so vivid in her mind.

Her hand went out to his, which was wrapped around the post. "Thank you for staying."

His hand seemed to tremble, and she wondered if she imagined it.

"You may not be grateful long," he replied shortly.

"You will stay, then?"

"A few days," he replied. "But the town won't like it. I'm usually not welcome."

"If Alex can hire you, I can," she answered defiantly.

"But Newton has money, and you . . . ?"

Again the implication was clear, and she knew she was flushing a bright red. She hoped the moonlight didn't reveal it, but she saw the glint in his eye and knew her hope was in vain.

Her thoughts turned to what had been nagging her, to the violent death that had occurred just hours earlier. "You won't have to fight Marsh Canton if you stay?" Her hand shook slightly as she posed the haunting question.

The glint was still in his eye. "A lot of folks been waiting for that."

"I've never seen anyone so . . . fast," she whispered.

His right hand went to his neck. "He's good. Aren't you going to ask me if I'm just as good?"

She didn't want to think of him that way. She preferred thinking of him hauling her poor bull Jupiter from the burning barn. "No," she whispered.

"That's what I do, you know," he persisted almost angrily. "I'm no hero like you want to believe. I'm a killer just like Canton. You want to know how many people I've killed?"

Her gaze was glued to his eyes, to the swirling, dangerous currents in them. She heard the raw self-contempt in his voice, but what he was saying didn't matter to her, not to the way she felt about him, not to the way she wanted to . . . touch and hold and . . .

"I was twelve when I first killed," he continued in the same voice. "Twelve. I found I was real good at it."

His eyes, filled with tormented memories and even rage, blazed directly at her. And she felt her need for him deepen, felt her heart pound with the compulsion to disprove his reason for self-derision.

But she couldn't move, and she had no words that wouldn't anger or hurt or sound naive and silly. That, she sensed, was what he was waiting for so he could have a reason to leave. The currents running between them were stronger than ever, and Lobo was willing her to say or do something to destroy it, but she was just as determined not to. Silence stretched between but something else too, something so strong that neither could back away.

If she'd offered compassion or sympathy, Lobo could have

broken through her hold on him. But she gave neither. Instead, he was warmed by the unfamiliar glow of understanding, of unquestioning acceptance. He basked in it, feeling whole for the first time that he could remember. All of a sudden he realized this was what he'd been searching for, not freedom but something so elusive he'd never been able to put a name to it.

And it was too late. His insides churned and twisted with pure agony as he realized that one indisputable fact. He carried too much trouble with him. His reputation, which he had so carefully nurtured, was a noose around his neck. The older he got, the more the rope tightened. He could live with that, but he couldn't live with the fact that it was also a noose around the neck of anyone foolish enough to care for him.

He forced himself to take a step back, to fight his way out of the moment's intimacy, one deeper than any he'd ever shared with a person, deeper than when he plunged his manhood into a woman. Christ!

"Lady, you should run like hell!" His voice was harsh, grating. "You and those kids don't need the kind of grief I bring."

She worried her lips as she sought for something to say, to somehow express her belief in him, but before she found the words, he spoke again.

"And I sure as hell don't need *you*." He emphasized the last word as if trying to convince himself, and once again he stepped back.

"Jess . . ."

His mouth seemed to soften for a moment, and he hesitated. But then his mouth firmed again, and his eyes turned hard. He bowed slightly, mockingly. "If I'm going to be of any use to you, ma'am, I'd better turn in."

He strolled lazily back to the barn and disappeared within, leaving Willow feeling desolate and alone.

HIGHLAND REBEL

BY STEPHANIE BARTLETT

Author of HIGHLAND JADE

Catriona Galbraith was a proud highland beauty who would do anything to stop a tyranical laird from possessing her homeland and heritage. Ian McLeod was the bold Texas rancher who swore to win Cat's love from the moment he laid eyes on the bewitching young woman. But Ian didn't know the dangerous secret that beckoned to Cat night after night: a secret that could sow the seeds of rebellion and destroy their passion.

*   *   *

Squares of yellow lamplight stained the snow in front of the church. Ian pulled his muffler tight against an icy gust as he followed Colin up the stone steps. The wind grew even colder after the winter sun went down.

Warm air, thick with the smells of wool and sweat, surrounded Ian as he sidled through the door. The interior droned with excited voices, all talking at once. Small wonder after the last two days.

Mindful of his height, he settled himself in the back pew. Colin patted his shoulder, then moved on up the aisle toward the front, where he could see and hear. For once Ian was glad to be an outlander. Without the old man around, the other crofters still ignored him for the most part, and that was fine with him. He didn't much want to talk to anybody anyhow. All they wanted to do was crow about their victories over the sheriff's men.

He wondered whatever had possessed the courts to send another officer the next day, trying to serve papers of some kind. Fin Lewis made short work of the man, a kid really. Tossed his papers in the muddy snow and escorted him to the edge of the estate at the point of his pike.

Ian rubbed at a smudge of soot staining his fingers. Most of the crofters wanted justice for themselves, but Fin liked to fight, bullying men who were outnumbered a hundred to one. Granddaddy always said there was one in every bunch.

He shrugged. At least they were on the same side, although he'd wager Fin was only concerned for himself. He didn't like the fella, didn't trust him at all. He only hoped he wouldn't ever have to depend on him.

Damn! The last thing he wanted to think about tonight was Lewis. Crossing his arms over his chest, he glanced around the room. The stone building was packed, every pew full to overflowing with men. Many of them even brought their families.

Gavin Nicolson smiled and waved from a few rows up. The man nudged the woman beside him. His daughter Belag. She turned and smiled back over her shoulder, but her cheeks crimsoned and she turned away when he tipped his hat. A pretty little thing with brown hair and dark eyes. She'd make some man a fine wife.

He tried to image himself with her, then shook his head to clear it. He knew he'd never love another woman, Catriona owned his heart, and she always would. Maybe someday his memories would dim enough so he could marry and have a family. But he didn't hold out much hope.

If only he could see Cat again, just for one night. He ached to put his arms around her, hold her, make love to her. His lips twisted into a bitter smile. She didn't love him, didn't want him, or she would have agreed to marry him. No, he might as well wish for a magic pony to ride him home to Texas across the clouds.

He wondered how things were at the Braes, with the poor crops and the hard winter. He missed Fergus and Jennet, Effie would be growing, and Geordie must be almost a man. It would be spring again soon. Two years since Granddaddy died. Two years since he met Catriona in the graveyard. Would his life ever be right again?

The voices around him subsided, bringing him out of his reverie. Dugald Purcell mounted the steps and took his place in the pulpit. "My friends, we have faced the enemy, and we have won!" A cheer echoed back from the rafters. Purcell went on, but Ian listened with only half an ear.

He shifted on the hard seat, trying to think how to go about settling these folks down. He could understand them being happy about running the sheriff out of town, but he figured they didn't know how dangerous it was to fight the law. And a lot of good it did him to warn Purcell, telling him what Campbell had said about the army; he just nodded and said, "Aye." And now he'd called another meeting.

A second figure moved up the pulpit steps, a woman, her head shrouded with a tartan shawl. Ian leaned forward. He'd seen her somewhere before. The image flashed through his mind, the woman who spoke with Purcell just before the fight at the bridge.

He caught the last of Purcell's words, something about a visitor who wanted to help plan their next actions. The slender figure stood beside the crofter. Facing the crowd, she lifted the shawl from her head, letting it drop to her shoulders. Black curls cascaded over her shoulders, and even from the back of the church, Ian could see her eyes were a deep blue. But it wasn't until she smiled that he knew for sure.

Catriona.

Catriona lay back on the musty coverlet and closed her eyes. Weariness weighed on her, the tension of the last few days and nights aching in every muscle. She was grateful for a bed and a room where she could be alone. On the edge of sleep, Ian's face floated before her.

Her body throbbed a bittersweet tune. She'd hungered for the sight of him for months, months with no word even to say he was still alive, still on Skye. Then tonight, as they ushered her into a church full of nervous crofters, there he stood.

She gave the speech Hugh helped her write before she left the Braes, rallying them to the cause and answering their questions. But she never forgot for a moment that he was there, sitting in the back, head and shoulders taller than the men around him. She tried not to look, but she couldn't keep her eyes away from him. The way his fine blond hair strayed across his forehead, shining in the lamplight, the way his handsome face eased into a smile and his eyes never strayed from her face as she talked. When the meeting ended and the crofters poured out the tall doors, she looked for him, but he'd vanished.

Cat rolled over and punched a hollow in the hard pillow. If only they could talk. Now, with them both fighting the lairds, he had to understand why she couldn't marry him and go to America, why she had to stay on Skye.

She tossed onto her back and stared up at the rafters. Tomorrow she'd find him, go to the forge and talk to him, tell him how much she missed him, how much she loved him. A smile curved her lips and she closed her eyes. Everything would be the way it was last spring.

A soft tapping startled her from a near-dream. It was late. Most of the guests at the lodge were asleep. She slid off the narrow bed and crept to the door, keeping her feet silent and her voice low. "Who is it?"

"Ian. Let me in."

Her pulse raced and she could scarcely catch her breath as she undid the bolt and pulled him into the room. In one move her arms went around his neck and her lips pressed his. Ian's love surrounded her, his hands traveling over her body. A delicious warmth swirled in her head and down her spine to end pulsing low in her belly.

Then Ian's hands cupped her shoulders and pushed her down onto the bed. She lay back and held up her arms to receive him.

He stood beside the bed, frowning down at her. "Cat, how can you do this?"

She sat up, her face flushed with disappointment and confusion. "Do what?"

"Risk your life traveling the countryside, stirring up trouble. Fighting the constables. I saw you in the crowd the other day. And the march to Dunvegan tomorrow. What will happen if you get caught?"

Anger kindled from the ashes of her longing. "Why, the same that'll happen if they catch you, I suppose."

His mouth opened, then snapped shut. "You don't

understand. The sergeant we chased out of here yesterday said the sheriff has asked for the army to come in."

The army. Purcell hadn't mentioned it. She bit her lip, trying to keep from shivering. "I hope they do," her voice sounded stronger than she felt.

He stared at her, his eyes wide. "A real war. Is that what you want?"

She tossed her head. "The eyes of the country are on Skye. The public is with us now. If they send the army against us, it can only make our case stronger."

He tossed up his hands and paced across the threadbare carpet. "And if they shoot people, will it be worth it then? Do you want to die?"

Cat swallowed before she answered. "Do you?" Her voice sounded hollow in her ears. She knew she didn't want to die, nor did she want him to die. Would the army really shoot to kill?

He stopped pacing and turned to face her, holding his clenched fists at his sides. "It's not the same thing. I'm a man."

"I've not forgotten what you are, but I see no difference in the risks we take." She pushed herself to her feet. "And you, what reason have you to fight the lairds? You're not even a proper Scotsman."

His full lips thinned to a hard line. "I'm a Macleod, same as the landlord. It's my duty to help make things right."

She took a step closer and planted her hands on her hips. "Aye, and I'm a Galbraith and a Macdonald. And I was born and bred a crofter, not a rich landowner from America."

The heat of his body reached out to her, but she fought the urge to touch him. Weariness settled over her again, and she looked away. It was no use—he'd never understand. "I've no more to say to you, so I'll thank you to leave now." She turned her back to him.

"Cat." His voice caressed her, and the longing pulsed deep in her belly. His hands slid down her shoulders and turned her toward him. Without a word he drew her into his arms and kissed her deep and long. Cat melted against him.

His mouth still clinging to hers, he lifted her and carried her to the bed.

She lay back, savoring the sweetness of his mouth on hers, the weight of his body pressing against her. His fingers fumbled at the buttons of her blouse, and then his hand cupped her breast, the work-roughened palm brushing her nipple. She gasped with pleasure as his lips followed his hand.

She traced the planes of his muscles, trailing her fingers down his chest. Trembling, she unfastened his trousers, slid her hands inside, and caressed the feverish hardness of his body.

He moaned and kissed her, pressing his lips against her mouth, her eyelids, her throat. His hands slid beneath her skirt, bunching the hem up around her waist. When his fingers smoothed the length of her thighs, caressing her secret pleasure, she arched against him in a fever of desire.

Unable to wait any longer, she tugged his trousers down over his buttocks and guided him inside her, closing her eyes and moaning as he filled her. She rose to meet him, wave after wave of pleasure washing through her, until she cried out, spilling over with delicious agony. Somewhere above her she heard him moan, and felt him collapse on top of her.

Without opening her eyes she slid her arms around him, holding his body against her. *Ian.* His name danced through her mind, making its own melody of love. Nothing else mattered.